The Survivors of th

Diary of J.R. Kazallc

Jules Verne

Alpha Editions

This edition published in 2024

ISBN : 9789366381466

Design and Setting By
Alpha Editions
www.alphaedis.com
Email - info@alphaedis.com

As per information held with us this book is in Public Domain.
This book is a reproduction of an important historical work. Alpha Editions uses the best technology to reproduce historical work in the same manner it was first published to preserve its original nature. Any marks or number seen are left intentionally to preserve its true form.

Contents

CHAPTER I. .... - 1 -

CHAPTER II. .... - 3 -

CHAPTER III. .... - 5 -

CHAPTER IV. .... - 6 -

CHAPTER V. .... - 10 -

CHAPTER VI. .... - 13 -

CHAPTER VII. .... - 15 -

CHAPTER VIII. .... - 18 -

CHAPTER IX. .... - 20 -

CHAPTER X. .... - 23 -

CHAPTER XI. .... - 26 -

CHAPTER XII. .... - 29 -

CHAPTER XIII. .... - 33 -

CHAPTER XIV. .... - 36 -

CHAPTER XV .... - 38 -

CHAPTER XVI. .... - 40 -

CHAPTER XVII.	- 44 -
CHAPTER XVIII.	- 46 -
CHAPTER XIX.	- 50 -
CHAPTER XX.	- 52 -
CHAPTER XXI.	- 55 -
CHAPTER XXII.	- 58 -
CHAPTER XXIII.	- 60 -
CHAPTER XXIV.	- 62 -
CHAPTER XXV.	- 64 -
CHAPTER XXVI.	- 67 -
CHAPTER XXVII.	- 70 -
CHAPTER XXVIII.	- 72 -
CHAPTER XXIX.	- 74 -
CHAPTER XXX.	- 76 -
CHAPTER XXXI.	- 78 -
CHAPTER XXXII.	- 80 -
CHAPTER XXXIII.	- 83 -
CHAPTER XXXIV.	- 86 -
CHAPTER XXXV.	- 89 -

CHAPTER XXXVI. .... - 92 -

CHAPTER XXXVII. .... - 94 -

CHAPTER XXXVIII. .... - 97 -

CHAPTER XXXIX. .... - 101 -

CHAPTER XL. .... - 104 -

CHAPTER XLI. .... - 106 -

CHAPTER XLII. .... - 109 -

CHAPTER XLIII. .... - 112 -

CHAPTER XLIV. .... - 116 -

CHAPTER XLV. .... - 119 -

CHAPTER XLVI. .... - 121 -

CHAPTER XLVII. .... - 124 -

CHAPTER XLVIII. .... - 126 -

CHAPTER XLIX. .... - 128 -

CHAPTER L. .... - 130 -

CHAPTER LI. .... - 131 -

CHAPTER LII. .... - 133 -

CHAPTER LIII. .... - 136 -

CHAPTER LIV. .... - 138 -

CHAPTER LV. ....- 140 -

CHAPTER LVI. ....- 142 -

CHAPTER LVII. ....- 143 -

CHAPTER I.

CHARLESTON, SEPTEMBER 27th, 1869.—It is high tide, and three o'clock in the afternoon when we leave the Battery-quay; the ebb carries us off shore, and as Captain Huntly has hoisted both main and top sails, the northerly breeze drives the "Chancellor" briskly across the bay. Fort Sumter ere long is doubled, the sweeping batteries of the mainland on our left are soon passed, and by four o'clock the rapid current of the ebbing tide has carried us through the harbour-mouth.

But as yet we have not reached the open sea; we have still to thread our way through the narrow channels which the surge has hollowed out amongst the sand-banks. The captain takes a south-west course, rounding the lighthouse at the corner of the fort; the sails are closely trimmed; the last sandy point is safely coasted, and at length, at seven o'clock in the evening; we are out free upon the wide Atlantic.

The "Chancellor" is a fine square-rigged three-master, of 900 tons burden, and belongs to the wealthy Liverpool firm of Laird Brothers. She is two years old, is sheathed and secured with copper, her decks being of teak, and the base of all her masts, except the mizzen, with all their fittings, being of iron. She is registered first class A I, and is now on her third voyage between Charleston and Liverpool. As she wended her way through the channels of Charleston harbour, it was the British flag that was lowered from her mast-head; but without colours at all, no sailor could have hesitated for a moment in telling her nationality,—for English she was, and nothing but English from her water-line upwards to the truck of her masts.

I must now relate how it happens that I have taken my passage on board the "Chancellor" on her return voyage to England. At present there is no direct steamship service between South Carolina and Great Britain, and all who wish to cross must go either northwards to New York or southwards to New Orleans. It is quite true that if I had chosen to start from New York I might have found plenty of vessels belonging to English, French, or Hamburg lines, any of which would have conveyed me by a rapid voyage to my destination; and it is equally true that if I had selected New Orleans for my embarkation I could readily have reached Europe by one of the vessels of the National Steam Navigation Company, which join the French Transatlantic line of Colon and Aspinwall. But it was fated to be otherwise.

One day, as I was loitering about the Charleston quays, my eye lighted upon this vessel. There was something about the "Chancellor" that pleased me, and a kind of involuntary impulse took me on board, where I found the internal arrangements perfectly comfortable. Yielding to the idea that a voyage in a sailing vessel had certain charms beyond the transit in a steamer, and reckoning that with wind and wave in my favour there would be little material difference in time; considering, moreover, that in these low latitudes the weather in early autumn is fine and unbroken, I came to my decision, and proceeded forthwith to secure my passage by this route to Europe.

Have I done right or wrong? Whether I shall have reason to regret my determination is a problem to be solved in the future. However, I will begin to record the incidents of our daily experience, dubious as I feel whether the lines of my chronicle will ever find a reader.

CHAPTER II.

SEPTEMBER 28th.—John Silas Huntly, the captain of the "Chancellor," has the reputation of being an experienced navigator of the Atlantic. He is a Scotchman, a native of Dundee, and is about fifty years of age. He is of middle height and slight build, and has a small head, which he has a habit of holding a little over his left shoulder. I do not pretend to be much of a physiognomist, but I am inclined to believe that my few hours' acquaintance with our captain has given me considerable insight into his character. That he is a good seaman and thoroughly understands his duties I could not for a moment venture to deny; but that he is a man of resolute temperament, or that he possesses the amount of courage that would render him, physically or morally, capable of coping with any great emergency, I confess I cannot believe. I observe a certain heaviness and dejection about his whole carriage. His wavering glances, the listless motions of his hands, and his slow, unsteady gait, all seem to me to indicate a weak and sluggish disposition. He does not appear as though he could be energetic enough ever to be stubborn; he never frowns, sets his teeth, or clenches his fist. There is something enigmatical about him; however, I shall study him closely and do what I can to understand the man who, as commander of a vessel, should be to those around him "second only to God."

Unless I am greatly mistaken there is another man on board who, if circumstances should require it, would take the more prominent position—I mean the mate. I have hitherto, however, had such little opportunity of observing his character, that I must defer saying more about him at present.

Besides the captain and this mate, whose name is Robert Curtis, our crew consists of Walter, the lieutenant, the boatswain, and fourteen sailors, all English or Scotch, making eighteen altogether, a number quite sufficient for working a vessel of 900 tons burden. Up to this time my sole experience of their capabilities is, that under the command of the mate, they brought us skillfully enough through the narrow channels of Charleston; and I have no reason to doubt but that they are well up to their work.

My list of the ship's officials is incomplete unless I mention Hobart, the steward, and Jynxstrop, the negro cook.

In addition to these, the "Chancellor" carries eight passengers, including myself. Hitherto, the bustle of embarkation, the arrangement of cabins, and all the variety of preparations inseparable from starting on a voyage for at least twenty or five-and-twenty days have precluded the formation of any acquaintanceships; but the monotony of the voyage, the close proximity into which we must be thrown, and the natural curiosity to know something of each other's affairs, will doubtless lead us in due time to an interchange of ideas. Two days have elapsed and I have not even seen all the passengers. Probably sea-sickness has prevented some of them from making their appearance at the common table. One thing, however, I do know; namely, that there are two ladies occupying the stern-cabins, the windows of which are in the aft-board of the vessel.

I have seen the ship's list and subjoin a list of the passengers. They are as follow:—Mr. and Mrs. Kear, Americans, of Buffalo. Miss Herbey, a young English lady, companion to Mrs. Kear. M. Letourneur and his son Andre, Frenchmen, of Havre. William Falsten, a Manchester engineer. John Ruby, a Cardiff merchant; and myself, J. R. Kazallon, of London.

CHAPTER III.

SEPTEMBER 29th.—Captain Huntly's bill of lading, that is to say, the document that describes the "Chancellor's" cargo and the conditions of transport, is couched in the following terms:—

"BRONSFIELD AND CO., AGENTS, CHARLESTON.

"I, John Silas Huntly, of Dundee, Scotland, commander of the ship 'Chancellor,' of about 900 tons burden, now at Charleston, do purpose, by the blessing of God, at the earliest convenient season, and by the direct route, to sail for the port of Liverpool, where I shall obtain my discharge. I do hereby acknowledge that I have received from you, Messrs. Bronsfield and Co., Commission Agents, Charleston, and have placed the same under the gun-deck of the aforesaid ship, seventeen hundred bales of cotton, of the estimated value of 26,000l., all in good condition, marked and numbered as in the margin; which goods I do undertake to transport to Liverpool, and there to deliver, free from injury (save only such injury as shall have been caused by the chances of the sea), to Messrs. Laird Brothers, or to their order, or to their representative, who shall on due delivery of the said freight pay me the sum of 2000l. inclusive, according to the charter-party and damages in addition, according to the usages and customs of the sea.

"And for the fulfillment of the above covenant, I have pledged and do pledge my person, my property, and my interest in the vessel aforesaid, with all its appurtenances. In witness whereof, I have signed three agreements, all of the same purport; on the condition that when the terms of one are accomplished, the other two shall be absolutely null and void.

"Given at Charleston, September 13th, 1869,

"J. S. HUNTLY."

From the foregoing document it will be understood that the "Chancellor" is conveying 1700 bales of cotton to Liverpool; that the shippers are Bronsfield, of Charleston, and the consignees are Laird Brothers, of Liverpool. The ship was constructed with the especial design of carrying cotton, and the entire hold, with the exception of a very limited space reserved for passengers' luggage, is closely packed with the bales, The lading was performed with the utmost care, each bale being pressed into its proper place by the aid of screw-jacks, so that the whole freight forms one solid and compact mass; not an inch of space is wasted, and the vessel is thus made capable of carrying her full complement of cargo.

CHAPTER IV.

SEPTEMBER 30th to OCTOBER 6th.—The "Chancellor" is a rapid sailer, and more than a match for many a vessel of the same dimensions. She scuds along merrily in the freshening breeze, leaving in her wake, far as the eye can reach, a long white line of foam as well defined as a delicate strip of lace stretched upon an azure ground.

The Atlantic is not visited by many gales, and I have every reason to believe that the rolling and pitching of the vessel no longer incommode any of the passengers, who are all more or less accustomed to the sea. A vacant seat at our table is now very rare; we are beginning to know something about each other, and our daily life, in consequence, is becoming somewhat less monotonous.

M. Letourneur, our French fellow-passenger, often has a chat with me. He is a fine tall man, about fifty years of age, with white hair and a grizzly beard. To say the truth, he looks older than he really is: his drooping head, his dejected manner, and his eye, ever and again suffused with tears, indicate that he is haunted by some deep and abiding sorrow. He never laughs; he rarely even smiles, and then only on his son: his countenance ordinarily bearing a look of bitterness tempered by affection, while his general expression is one of caressing tenderness. It excites an involuntary commiseration to learn that M. Letourneur is consuming himself by exaggerated reproaches on account of the infirmity of an afflicted son.

Andre Letourneur is about twenty years of age, with a gentle, interesting countenance, but, to the irrepressible grief of his father, is a hopeless cripple. His left leg is miserably deformed, and he is quite unable to walk without the assistance of a stick. It is obvious that the father's life is bound up with that of his son; his devotion is unceasing; every thought, every glance is for Andre; he seems to anticipate his most trifling wish, watches his slightest movement, and his arm is ever ready to support or otherwise assist the child whose sufferings he more than shares.

M. Letourneur seems to have taken a peculiar fancy to myself, and constantly talks about Andre. This morning, in the course of conversation, I said,—

"You have a good son, M. Letourneur. I have just been talking to him. He is a most intelligent young man."

"Yes, Mr. Kazallon," replied M. Letourneur, brightening up into a smile, "his afflicted frame contains a noble mind. He is like his mother, who died at his birth."

"He is full of reverence and love for you, sir," I remarked.

"Dear boy!" muttered the father half to himself. "Ah, Mr. Kazallon," he continued, "you do not know what it is to a father to have a son a cripple, beyond hope of cure."

"M. Letourneur," I answered, "you take more than your share of the affliction which has fallen upon you and your son. That M. Andre is entitled to the very greatest commiseration no one can deny; but you should remember, that after all a physical infirmity is not so hard to bear as mental grief. Now, I have watched your son pretty closely, and unless I am much mistaken there is nothing, that troubles him so much as the sight of your own sorrow."

"But I never let him see it," he broke in hastily. "My sole thought is how to divert him. I have discovered, that in spite of his physical weakness, he delights in travelling; so for the last few years we have been constantly on the move. We first went all over Europe, and are now returning from visiting the principal places in the United States. I never allowed my son to go to college, but instructed him entirely myself, and these travels, I hope, will serve to complete his education. He is very intelligent, and has a lively imagination, and I am sometimes tempted to hope that in contemplating the wonders of nature he forgets his own infirmity."

"Yes, sir, of course he does," I assented.

"But," continued M. Letourneur, taking my hand, "although, perhaps, HE may forget, I can never forget. Ah, sir, do you suppose that Andre can ever forgive his parents for bringing him into the world a cripple?"

The remorse of the unhappy father was very distressing, and I was about to say a few kind words of sympathy when Andre himself made his appearance. M. Letourneur hastened toward him and assisted him up the few steep steps that led to the poop.

As soon as Andre was comfortably seated on one of the benches, and his father had taken his place by his side, I joined them, and we fell into conversation upon ordinary topics, discussing the various points of the "Chancellor," the probable length of the passage, and the different details of our life on board. I find that M. Letourneur's estimate of Captain Huntly's character very much coincided with my own, and that, like me, he is impressed with the man's undecided manner and sluggish appearance. Like me, too, he has formed a very favourable opinion of Robert Curtis, the mate, a man of about thirty years of age, of great muscular power, with a frame and a will that seem ever ready for action.

Whilst we were still talking of him, Curtis himself came on deck, and as I watched his movements I could not help being struck with his physical development; his erect and easy carriage, his fearless glance and slightly contracted brow all betokened a man of energy, thoroughly endowed with the calmness and courage that are indispensable to the true sailor. He seems a kind-hearted fellow, too, and is always ready to assist and amuse young Letourneur, who evidently enjoys his company. After he had scanned the weather and examined the trim of the sails, he joined our party and proceeded to give us some information about those of our fellow-passengers with whom at present we have made but slight acquaintance.

Mr. Kear, the American, who is accompanied by his wife, has made a large fortune in the petroleum springs in the United States. He is a man of about fifty, a most uninteresting companion, being overwhelmed with a sense of his own wealth and importance, and consequently supremely indifferent to all around him. His hands are always in his pockets, and the chink of money seems to follow him wherever he goes. Vain and conceited, a fool as well as an egotist, he struts about like a peacock showing its plumage, and to borrow the words of the physiognomist Gratiolet, "il se flaire, il se savoure, il se goute." Why he should have taken his passage on board a mere merchant vessel instead of enjoying the luxuries of a Transatlantic steamer, I am altogether at a loss to explain.

The wife is an insignificant, insipid woman, of about forty years of age. She never reads, never talks, and I believe I am not wrong in saying, never thinks. She seems to look without seeing, and listen without hearing, and her sole occupation consists in giving her orders to her companion, Miss Herbey, a young English girl of about twenty.

Miss Herbey is extremely pretty. Her complexion is fair and her eyes deep blue, whilst her pleasing countenance is altogether free from that insignificance of feature which is not unfrequently alleged to be characteristic of English beauty. Her mouth would be charming if she ever smiled, but exposed as she is to the ridiculous whims and fancies of a capricious mistress, her lips rarely relax from their ordinary grave expression. Yet humiliating as her position must be, she never utters a word of open complaint, but quietly and gracefully performs her duties accepting without a murmur the paltry salary which the bumptious petroleum-merchant condescends to allow her.

The Manchester engineer, William Falsten, looks like a thorough Englishman. He has the management of some extensive hydraulic works in South Carolina, and is now on his way to Europe to obtain some improved apparatus, and more especially to visit the mines worked by centrifugal force, belonging to the firm of Messrs. Cail. He is forty-five years of age, with all his interests so entirely absorbed by his machinery that he seems to have neither a thought nor a care beyond his mechanical calculations. Once let him engage you in conversation, and there is no chance of escape; you have no help for it but to listen as patiently as you can until he has completed the explanation of his designs.

The last of our fellow-passengers, Mr. Ruby, is the type of a vulgar tradesman. Without any originality or magnanimity in his composition, he has spent twenty years of his life in mere buying and selling, and as he has generally contrived to do business at a profit, he has realized a considerable fortune. What he is going to do with the money, he does not seem able to say: his ideas do not go beyond retail trade, his mind having been so long closed to all other impressions that it appears incapable of thought or reflection on any subject besides. Pascal says, "L'homme est visiblement fait pour penser. C'est toute sa dignite et tout-son merite;" but to Mr. Ruby the phrase seems altogether inapplicable.

CHAPTER V.

OCTOBER 7th.—This is the tenth day since we left Charleston, and I should think our progress has been very rapid. Robert Curtis, the mate, with whom I continue to have many a friendly chat, informed me that we could not be far off Cape Hatteras in the Bermudas; the ship's bearings, he said were lat. 32deg. 20min. N. and long. 64deg. 50min. W., so that he had every reason to believe that we should sight St. George's Island before night.

"The Bermudas!" I exclaimed. "But how is it we are off the Bermudas? I should have thought that a vessel sailing from Charleston to Liverpool, would have kept northwards, and have followed the track of the Gulf Stream."

"Yes, indeed; sir," replied Curtis, "that is the usual course; but you see that this time the captain hasn't chosen to take it."

"But why not?" I persisted.

"That's not for me to say, sir; he ordered us eastwards, and eastwards we go."

"Haven't you called his attention to it?" I inquired.

Curtis acknowledged that he had already pointed out what an unusual route they were taking, but that the captain had said that he was quite aware what he was about. The mate made no further remark; but the knit of his brow, as he passed his hand mechanically across his forehead, made me fancy that he was inclined to speak out more strongly.

"All very well, Curtis," I said, "but I don't know what to think about trying new routes. Here we are at the 7th of October, and if we are to reach Europe before the bad weather sets in, I should suppose there is not a day to be lost."

"Right, sir, quite right; there is not a day to be lost."

Struck by his manner, I ventured to add, "Do you mind, Mr. Curtis giving me your honest opinion of Captain Huntly?"

He hesitated a moment, and then replied shortly, "He is my captain, sir."

This evasive answer of course put an end to any further interrogation on my part, but it only set me thinking the more.

Curtis was not mistaken. At about three o'clock the lookout man sung out that there was land to windward, and descried what seemed as if it might be a line of smoke in the north-east horizon. At six, I went on deck with M. Letourneur and his son, and we could then distinctly make out the low group of the Bermudas, encircled by their formidable chain of breakers.

"There," said Andre Letourneur to me, as we stood gazing at the distant land, "there lies the enchanted Archipelago, sung by your poet Moore. The exile Waller, too, as long ago as 1643, wrote an enthusiastic panegyric on the islands, and I have been told that at one time English ladies would wear no other bonnets than such as were made of the leaves of the Bermuda palm."

"Yes," I replied, "the Bermudas were all the rage in the seventeenth century, although latterly they have fallen into comparative oblivion."

"But let me tell you, M. Andre," interposed Curtis, who had as usual joined our party, "that although poets may rave, and be as enthusiastic as they like about these islands, sailors will tell a different tale. The hidden reefs that lie in a semicircle about two or three leagues from shore make the attempt to land a very dangerous piece of business. And another thing, I know. Let the natives boast as they will about their splendid climate, they, are visited by the most frightful hurricanes. They get the fag-end of the storms that rage over the Antilles; and the fag-end of a storm is like the tail of a whale; it's just the strongest bit of it. I don't think you'll find a sailor listening much to your poets,—your Moores, and your Wallers."

"No, doubt you are right, Mr. Curtis," said Andre, smiling, "but poets are like proverbs; you can always find one to contradict another. Although Waller and Moore have chosen to sing the praises of the Bermudas, it has been supposed that Shakspeare was depicting them in the terrible scenes that are found in 'The Tempest.'"

The whole vicinity of these islands is beyond a question extremely perilous to mariners. Situated between the Antilles and Nova Scotia, the Bermudas have ever since their discovery belonged to the English, who have mainly used them for a military station. But this little archipelago, comprising some hundred and fifty different isles and islets, is destined to increase, and that, perhaps, on a larger scale than has yet been anticipated. Beneath the waves there are madrepores, in infinity of number, silently but ceaselessly pursuing their labours; and with time, that fundamental element in nature's workings, who shall tell whether these may not gradually build up island after island, which shall unite and form another continent?

I may mention that there was not another of our fellow-passengers who took the trouble to come on deck and give a glance at this strange cluster of islands. Miss Herbey, it is true, was making an attempt to join us, but she had barely reached the poop, when Mrs. Kear's languid voice was heard recalling her for some trifling service to her side.

CHAPTER VI.

OCTOBER 8th to OCTOBER 13th.—The wind is blowing hard from the north-east; and the "Chancellor" under low-reefed top-sail and fore-sail, and labouring against a heavy sea, has been obliged to be brought ahull. The joists and girders all creak again until one's teeth are set on edge. I am the only passenger not remaining below; but I prefer being on deck notwithstanding the driving rain, fine as dust, which penetrates to my very skin. We have been driven along in this fashion for the best part of two days; the "stiffish breeze" has gradually freshened into "a gale;" the top-gallants have been lowered, and, as I write, the wind is blowing with a velocity of fifty or sixty miles an hour. Although the "Chancellor" has many good points, her drift is considerable, and we have been carried far to the south we can only guess at our precise position, as the cloudy atmosphere entirely precludes us from taking the sun's altitude.

All along throughout this period, my fellow-passengers are totally ignorant of the extraordinary course that we are taking England lies to the NORTH-EAST, yet we are sailing directly SOUTH-EAST, and Robert Curtis owns that he is quite bewildered; he cannot comprehend why the captain, ever since this north-easterly gale has been blowing, should persist in allowing the ship to drive to the south, instead of tacking to the north-west until she gets into better quarters.

I was alone with Curtis to-day upon the poop, and could not help saying to him "Curtis, is your captain mad?"

"Perhaps, sir, I might be allowed to ask what YOU think upon that matter," was his cautious reply.

"Well to say the truth," I answered, "I can hardly tell; but I confess there is every now and then a wandering in his eye, and an odd look on his face that I do not like. Have you ever sailed with him before?"

"No; this is our first voyage together. Again last night I spoke to him about the route we were taking, but he only said he knew all about it, and that it was all right."

"What do Lieutenant Walter and your boatswain think of it all?" I inquired.

"Think; why they think just the same as I do," replied the mate; "but if the captain chooses to take the ship to China we should obey his orders."

"But surely," I exclaimed, "there must be some limit to your obedience! Suppose the man is actually mad, what then?"

"If he should be mad enough, Mr. Kazallon, to bring the vessel into any real danger, I shall know what to do."

With this assurance I am forced to be content. Matters, however, have taken a different turn to what I bargained for when I took my passage on board the "Chancellor." The weather has become worse and worse. As I have already said, the ship under her large low-reefed top-sail and fore stay-sail has been brought ahull, that is to say, she copes directly with the wind, by presenting her broad bows to the sea; and so we go on still drift, drift, continually to the south.

How southerly our course has been is very apparent; for upon the night of the 11th we fairly entered upon that portion of the Atlantic which is known as the Sargassos Sea. An extensive tract of water is this, enclosed by the warm current of the Gulf Stream, and thickly covered with the wrack, called by the Spaniards "sargasso," the abundance of which so seriously impeded the progress of Columbus's vessels on his first voyage across the ocean.

Each morning at daybreak the Atlantic has presented an aspect so remarkable, that at my solicitation, M. Letourneur and his son have ventured upon deck to witness the unusual spectacle. The squally gusts make the metal shrouds vibrate like harp-strings; and unless we were on our guard to keep our clothes wrapped tightly to us, they would have been torn off our backs in shreds. The scene presented to our eyes is one of strangest interest. The sea, carpeted thickly with masses of prolific fucus, is a vast unbroken plain of vegetation, through which the vessel makes her way as a plough. Long strips of seaweed caught up by the wind become entangled in the rigging, and hang between the masts in festoons of verdure; whilst others, varying from two to three hundred feet in length, twine themselves up to the very mast-heads, from whence they float like streaming pendants. For many hours now, the "Chancellor" has been contending with this formidable accumulation of algae; her masts are circled with hydrophytes; her rigging is wreathed everywhere with creepers, fantastic as the untrammelled tendrils of a vine, and as she works her arduous course, there are times when I can only compare her to an animated grove of verdure making its mysterious way over some illimitable prairie.

CHAPTER VII.

OCTOBER 14th.—At last we are free from the sea of vegetation, the boisterous gale has moderated into a steady breeze, the sun is shining brightly, the weather is warm and genial, and thus, two reefs in her top-sails, briskly and merrily sails the "Chancellor."

Under conditions so favourable, we have been able to take the ship's bearings: our latitude, we find, is 21deg. 33min. N., our longitude 50deg. 17min. W.

Incomprehensible altogether is the conduct of Captain Huntly. Here we are, already more than ten degrees south of the point from which, we started, and yet still we are persistently following a south-easterly course! I cannot bring myself to the conclusion that the man is mad. I have had various conversations with him: he has always spoken rationally and sensibly. He shows no tokens of insanity. Perhaps his case is one of those in which insanity is partial, and where the mania is of a character which extends only to the matters connected with his profession. Yet it is unaccountable.

I can get nothing out of Curtis; he listens coldly whenever I allude to the subject, and only repeats what he has said before, that nothing short of an overt act of madness on the part of the captain could induce him to supersede the captain's authority and that the imminent peril of the ship could alone justify him in taking so decided a measure.

Last evening I went to my cabin about eight o'clock, and after an hour's reading by the light of my cabin-lamp, I retired to my berth and was soon asleep. Some hours later I was aroused by an unaccustomed noise on deck. There were heavy footsteps hurrying to and fro, and the voices of the men were loud and eager, as if the crew were agitated by some strange disturbance. My first impression was, that some tacking had been ordered which rendered it needful to fathom the yards; but the vessel continuing to lie to starboard convinced me that this was not the origin of the commotion, I was curious to know the truth, and made all haste I could to go on deck; but before I was ready, the noise had ceased. I heard Captain Huntly return to his cabin, and accordingly I retired again to my own berth. Whatever may have been the meaning of the manoeuvre, I cannot tell; it did not seem to have resulted in any improvement in the ship's pace; still it must be owned there was not much wind to speed us along.

At six o'clock this morning I mounted the poop and made as keen a scrutiny as I could of everything on board. Everything appeared as usual.

The "Chancellor" was running on the larboard tack, and carried low-sails, top-sails, and gallant-sails. Well braced she was; and under a fresh, but not uneasy breeze, was making no less than eleven knots an hour.

Shortly afterwards M. Letourneur and Andre came an deck. The young man enjoyed the early morning air, laden with its briny fragrance, and I assisted him to mount the poop. In answer to my inquiry as to whether they had been disturbed by any bustle in the night, Andre replied that he did not wake at all, and had heard nothing.

"I am glad, my boy," said his father, "that you have slept so soundly. I heard the noise of which Mr. Kazallon speaks. It must have; been about three o'clock this morning, and it seemed to me as though they were shouting. I thought I heard them say, 'Here, quick, look to the hatches!' but as nobody was called up, I presumed that nothing serious was the matter."

As he spoke I cast my eye at the panel-slides, which fore and aft of the main-mast open into the hold. They seemed to be all close as usual, but I now observed for the first time that they were covered with heavy tarpauling. Wondering; in my own mind what could be the reason for these extra precautions I did not say anything to M. Letourneur, but determined to wait until the mate should come on watch, when he would doubtless give me, I thought, an explanation of the mystery.

The sun rose gloriously, with every promise of a fine dry day. The waning moon was yet above the western horizon, for as it still wants three days to her last quarter she does not set until 10.57 am. On consulting my almanac, I find that there will be a new moon on the 24th, and that on that day, little as it may affect us here in mid ocean, the phenomenon of the high sygyzian tides will take place on the shores of every continent and island.

At the breakfast hour M. Letourneur and Andre went below for a cup of tea, and I remained on the poop alone. As I expected, Curtis appeared, that he might relieve Lieutenant Walter of the watch. I advanced to meet him, but before he even wished me good morning, I saw him cast a quick and searching glance upon the deck, and then, with a slightly contracted brow, proceed to examine the state of the weather and the trim of the sails.

"Where is Captain Huntly?" he said to Walter.

"I have seen nothing of him," answered the lieutenant "is there anything fresh up?"

"Nothing, whatever," was the curt reply.

They then conversed for a few moments in an undertone, and I could see that Walter by his gesture gave a negative answer to some question which the mate had asked him. "Send me the boatswain, Walter," said Curtis aloud as the lieutenant moved away.

The boatswain immediately appeared, and another conversation was carried on in whispers. The man repeatedly shook his head as he replied to Curtis's inquiries, and then, in obedience to orders, called the men who were on watch, and made them plentifully water the tarpauling that covered the great hatchway.

Curious to fathom the mystery I went up to Curtis and began to talk to him upon ordinary topics, hoping that he would himself introduce the subject that was uppermost in my mind; finding, however, that he did not allude to it; I asked him point blank.

"What was the matter in the night, Curtis?"

He looked at me steadily, but made no reply.

"What was it?" I repeated. "M. Letourneur and myself were both of us disturbed by a very unusual commotion overhead."

"Oh, a mere nothing," he said at length; "the man at the helm had made a false move, and we had to pipe hands to brace the ship a bit; but it was soon all put to rights. It was nothing, nothing at all."

I said no more; but I cannot resist the impression that Robert Curtis has not acted with me in his usual straightforward manner.

CHAPTER VIII.

OCTOBER 15th to OCTOBER 18th.—The wind is still in the north-east. There is no change in the "Chancellor's" course, and to an unprejudiced eye all would appear to be going on as usual. But I have an uneasy consciousness that something is not quite right. Why should the hatchways be so hermetically closed as though a mutinous crew was imprisoned between decks? I cannot help thinking too that there is something in the sailors so constantly standing in groups and breaking off their talk so suddenly whenever we approach; and several times I have caught the word "hatches" which arrested M. Letourneur's attention on the night of the disturbance.

On the 15th, while I was walking on the forecastle, I overheard one of the sailors, a man named Owen say to his mates,—

"Now I just give you all warning that I am not going to wait until the last minute. Every one for himself, say I."

"Why, what do you mean to do?" asked Jynxstrop, the cook.

"Pshaw!" said Owen, "do you suppose that longboats were only made for porpoises?"

Something at that moment occurred to interrupt the conversation, and I heard no more. It occurred to me whether there was not some conspiracy among the crew, of which probably Curtis had already detected the symptoms. I am quite aware that some sailors are most rebelliously disposed, and require to be ruled with a rod of iron.

Yesterday and to-day I have observed Curtis remonstrating somewhat vehemently with Captain Huntly, but there is no obvious result arising from their interviews; the Captain apparently being bent upon some purpose, of which it is only too manifest that the mate decidedly disapproves.

Captain Huntly is undoubtedly labouring under strong nervous excitement; and M. Letourneur has more than once remarked how silent he has become at meal-times; for although Curtis continually endeavours to start some subject of general interest, yet neither Mr. Falsten, Mr. Kear, nor Mr. Ruby are the men to take it up, and consequently the conversation flags hopelessly, and soon drops. The passengers too are now, with good cause, beginning to murmur at the length of the voyage, and Mr. Kear, who considers that the very elements ought to yield to his convenience, lets the captain know by his consequential and haughty manner that he holds him responsible for the delay.

During the course of yesterday the mate gave repeated orders for the deck to be watered again and again, and although as a general rule this is a business which is done, once for all, in the early morning, the crew did not utter a word of complaint at the additional work thus imposed upon them. The tarpaulins on the hatches have thus been kept continually wet, so that their close and heavy texture is rendered quite impervious to the air, The "Chancellor's" pumps afford a copious supply of water, so that I should not suppose that even the daintiest and most luxurious craft belonging to an aristocratic yacht-club was ever subject to a more thorough scouring. I tried to reconcile myself to the belief that it was the high temperature of the tropical regions upon which we are entering, that rendered such extra sousings a necessity, and recalled to my recollection how, during the night of the 13th, I had found the atmosphere below deck so stifling that in spite of the heavy swell I was obliged to open the porthole of my cabin, on the starboard side, to get a breath of air.

This morning at daybreak I went on deck. The sun had scarcely risen, and the air was fresh and cool, in strange contrast to the heat which below the poop had been quite oppressive. The sailors as usual were washing the deck, A great sheet of water, supplied continuously by the pumps was rolling in tiny wavelets, and escaping now to starboard, now to larboard through the scupper-holes. After watching the men for a while as they ran about bare-footed, I could not resist the desire to join them, so taking off my shoes and stockings I proceeded to dabble in the flowing water.

Great was my amazement to find the deck perfectly hot to my feet! Curtis heard my exclamation of surprise, and before I could put my thoughts into words, said,—

"Yes! there is fire on board!"

CHAPTER IX.

OCTOBER 19th.—Everything, then, is clear. The uneasiness of the crew, their frequent conferences, Owen's mysterious words, the constant scourings of the deck and the oppressive heat of the cabins which had been noticed even by my fellow-passengers, all are explained.

After his grave communication, Curtis remained silent. I shivered with a thrill of horror; a calamity the most terrible that can befall a voyager stared me in the face, and it was some seconds before I could recover sufficient composure to inquire when the fire was first discovered.

"Six days ago," replied the mate.

"Six days ago!" I exclaimed; "why, then, it was that night."

"Yes," he said, interrupting me; "it was the night you heard the disturbance upon deck. The men on watch noticed a slight smoke issuing from the large hatchway and immediately called Captain Huntly and myself. We found beyond all doubt, that the cargo was on fire, and what was worse, that there was no possibility of getting at the seat of the combustion. What could we do? Why; we took the only precaution that was practicable under the circumstances, and resolved most carefully to exclude every breath of air from penetrating into the hold, For some time I hoped that we had been successful. I thought that the fire was stifled; but during the last three days there is every reason to make us know that it has been gaining strength. Do what we will, the deck gets hotter and hotter, and unless it were kept constantly wet, it would be unbearable to the feet. But I am glad, Mr. Kazallon," he added; "that you have made the discovery. It is better that you should know it."

I listened in silence, I was now fully aroused to the gravity of the situation and thoroughly comprehended how we were in the very face of a calamity which it seemed that no human power could avert.

"Do you know what has caused the fire?" I presently inquired.

"It probably arose," he answered, "from the spontaneous combustion of the cotton. The case is rare, but it is far from unknown. Unless the cotton is perfectly dry when it is shipped, its confinement in a damp or ill-ventilated hold will sometimes cause it to ignite; and I have no doubt it is this that has brought about our misfortune."

"But after all," I said, "the cause matters very little. Is there no remedy? Is there nothing to be done?"

"Nothing; Mr. Kazallon," he said. "As I told you before, we have adopted the only possible measure within our power to check the fire. At one time I thought of knocking a hole in the ship's timbers just on her waterline, and letting in just as much water as the pumps could afterwards get rid of again; but we found the combustion was right in the middle of the cargo and that we should be obliged to flood the entire hold before we could get at the right place. That scheme consequently was no good. During the night, I had the deck bored in various places and water poured down through the holes; but that again seemed all of no use. There is only one thing that can be done; we must persevere in excluding most carefully every breath of outer air, so that perhaps the conflagration deprived of oxygen may smoulder itself out. That is our only hope."

"But, you say the fire is increasing?"

"Yes; and that shows that in spite of all our care there is some aperture which we have not been able to discover, by which, somehow or other, air gets into the hold."

"Have you ever heard of a vessel surviving such circumstances?" I asked.

"Yes, Mr. Kazallon," said Curtis; "it is not at all an unusual thing for ships laden with cotton to arrive at Liverpool or Havre with a portion of their cargo consumed; and I have myself known more than one captain run into port with his deck scorching his very feet, and who, to save his vessel and the remainder of his freight has been compelled to unload with the utmost expedition. But, in such cases, of course the fire has been more or less under control throughout the voyage; with us, it is increasing day by day, and I tell you I am convinced there is an aperture somewhere which has escaped our notice."

"But would it not be advisable for us to retrace our course, and make for the nearest land?"

"Perhaps it would," he answered. "Walter and I, and the boatswain, are going to talk the matter over seriously with the captain to-day. But, between ourselves, I have taken the responsibility upon myself; I have already changed the tack to the south-west; we are now straight before the wind, and consequently we are sailing towards the coast."

"I need hardly ask," I added; "whether any of the other passengers are at all aware of the imminent danger in which we are placed."

"None of them," he said; "not in the least; and I hope you will not enlighten them. We don't want terrified women and cowardly men to add to our embarrassment; the crew are under orders to keep a strict silence on the subject. Silence is indispensable."

I promised to keep the matter a profound secret, as I fully entered into Curtis's views as to the absolute necessity for concealment.

CHAPTER X.

OCTOBER 20th AND 21st.—The "Chancellor" is now crowded with all the canvas she can carry, and at times her top-masts threaten to snap with the pressure. But Curtis is ever on the alert; he never leaves his post beside the man at the helm, and without compromising the safety of the vessel, he contrives by tacking to the breeze, to urge her on at her utmost speed.

All day long on the 20th, the passengers were assembled on the poop. Evidently they found the heat of the cabins painfully oppressive, and most of them lay stretched upon benches and quietly enjoyed the gentle rolling of the vessel. The increasing heat of the deck did not reveal itself to their well-shod feet and the constant scouring of the boards did not excite any suspicion in their torpid minds. M. Letourneur, it is true, did express his surprise that the crew of an ordinary merchant vessel should be distinguished by such extraordinary cleanliness, but as I replied to him in a very casual tone, he passed no further remark. I could not help regretting that I had given Curtis my pledge of silence, and longed intensely to communicate the melancholy secret to the energetic Frenchman; for at times when I reflect upon the eight-and-twenty victims who may probably, only too soon, be a prey to the relentless flames, my heart seems ready to burst.

The important consultation between captain, mate, lieutenant, and boatswain has taken place. Curtis has confided the result to me. He says that Huntly, the captain, is completely demoralized; he has lost all power and energy; and practically leaves the command of the ship to him. It is now certain the fire is beyond control, and that sooner or later it will burst out in full violence The temperature of the crew's quarters has already become almost unbearable. One solitary hope remained; it is that we may reach the shore before the final catastrophe occurs. The Lesser Antilles are the nearest land; and although they are some five or six hundred miles away, if the wind remains north-east there is yet a chance of reaching them in time.

Carrying royals and studding-sails, the "Chancellor" during the last four-and-twenty hours has held a steady course. M. Letourneur is the only one of all the passengers who has remarked the change of tack; Curtis however, has set all speculation on his part to rest by telling him that he wanted to get ahead of the wind, and that he was tacking to the west to catch a favourable current.

To-day, the 21st, all has gone on as usual; and as far as the observation of the passengers has reached, the ordinary routine has been undisturbed. Curtis indulges the hope even yet that by excluding the air, the fire may be stifled before it ignites the general cargo; he has hermetically closed every accessible aperture, and has even taken the precaution of plugging the orifices of the pumps, under the impression that their suction-tubes, running as they do to the bottom of the hold, may possibly be channels for conveying some molecules of air. Altogether, he considers it a good sign that the combustion has not betrayed itself by some external issue of smoke.

The day would have passed without any incident worth recording if I had not chanced to overhear a fragment of a conversation which demonstrated that our situation hitherto precarious enough, had now become most appalling.

As I was sitting on the poop, two of my fellow-passengers, Falsten, the engineer, and Ruby, the merchant whom I had observed to be often in company, were engaged in conversation almost close to me. What they said was evidently not intended for my hearing, but my attention was directed towards them by some very emphatic gestures of dissatisfaction on the part of Falsten, and I could not forbear listening to what followed.

"Preposterous! shameful!" exclaimed Falsten; "nothing could be more imprudent."

"Pooh! pooh!" replied Ruby; "it's all right; it is not the first time I have done it."

"But don't you know that any shock at any time might cause an explosion?"

"Oh, it's all properly secured," said Ruby, "tight enough; I have no fears on that score, Mr. Falsten."

"But why," asked Falsten, "did you not inform the captain?"

"Just because if I had informed him, he would not have taken the case on board."

The wind dropped for a few seconds; and for a brief interval I could not catch what passed; but I could see that Falsten continued to remonstrate, whilst Ruby answered by shrugging his shoulders. At length I heard Falsten say,—

"Well, at any rate the captain must be informed of this, and the package shall be thrown overboard. I don't want, to be blown up."

I started. To what could the engineer be alluding? Evidently he had not the remotest suspicion that the cargo was already on fire. In another moment the words "picrate of potash" brought me to my feet? and with an involuntary impulse I rushed up to Ruby, and seized him by the shoulder.

"Is there picrate of potash on board?" I almost shrieked.

"Yes," said Falsten, "a case containing thirty pounds."

"Where is it?" I cried.

"Down in the hold, with the cargo."

CHAPTER XI.

What my feelings were I cannot describe; but it was hardly in terror so much as with a kind of resignation that I made my way to Curtis on the forecastle, and made him aware that the alarming character of our situation was now complete, as there was enough explosive matter on board to blow up a mountain. Curtis received the information as coolly as it was delivered, and after I had made him acquainted with all the particulars said,—

"Not a word of this must be mentioned to any one else, Mr. Kazallon, where is Ruby now?"

"On the poop," I said.

"Will you then come with me, sir?"

Ruby and Falsten were sitting just as I had left them. Curtis walked straight up to Ruby, and asked him whether what he had been told was true.

"Yes, quite true," said Ruby, complacently, thinking that the worst that could befall him would be that he might be convicted of a little smuggling.

I observed that Curtis was obliged for a moment or two to clasp his hands tightly together behind his back to prevent himself from seizing the unfortunate passenger by the throat; but suppressing his indignation, he proceeded quietly, though sternly, to interrogate him about the facts of the case. Ruby only confirmed what I had already told him. With characteristic Anglo-Saxon incautiousness he had brought on board with the rest of his baggage, a case containing no less than thirty pounds of picrate, and had allowed the explosive matter to be stowed in the hold with as little compunction as a Frenchman would feel in smuggling a single bottle of wine. He had not informed the captain of the dangerous nature of the contents of the package, because he was perfectly aware that he would have been refused permission to bring the package on board.

"Any way," he said, with a shrug of his shoulders, "you can't hang me for it; and if the package gives you so much concern, you are quite at liberty to throw it into the sea. My luggage is insured."

I was beside myself with fury, and not being endowed with Curtis's reticence and self-control, before he could interfere to stop me, I cried out,—

"You fool! don't you know that there is fire on board?"

In an instant I regretted my words. Most earnestly I wished them unuttered, But it was too late: their effect upon Ruby was electrical. He was paralyzed with terror his limbs stiffened convulsively; his eye was dilated; he gasped for breath, and was speechless. All of a sudden he threw up his arms and, as though he momentarily expected an explosion, he darted down from the poop, and paced frantically up and down the deck, gesticulating like a madman, and shouting,—

"Fire on board! Fire! Fire!"

On hearing the outcry, all the crew, supposing that the fire had now in reality broken out, rushed on deck; the rest of the passengers soon joined them, and the scene that ensued was one of the utmost confusion. Mrs. Kear fell down senseless on the deck, and her husband, occupied in looking after himself, left her to the tender mercies of Miss Herbey. Curtis endeavoured to silence Ruby's ravings, whilst I, in as few words as I could, made M. Letourneur aware of the extent to which the cargo was on fire. The father's first thought was for Andre but the young man preserved an admirable composure, and begged his father not to be alarmed, as the danger was not immediate. Meanwhile the sailors had loosened all the tacklings of the long-boat; and were preparing to launch it, when Curtis's voice was heard peremptorily bidding them to desist; he assured them that the fire had made no further progress; that Mr. Ruby had been unduly excited and not conscious of what he had said; and he pledged his word that when the right moment should arrive he would allow them all to leave the ship; but that moment, he said, had not yet come.

At the sound of a voice which they had learned to honour and respect, the crew paused in their operations, and the long-boat remained suspended in its place. Fortunately, even Ruby himself in the midst of his ravings, had not dropped a word about the picrate that had been deposited in the hold; for although the mate had a power over the sailors that Captain Huntly had never possessed, I feel certain that if the true state of the case had been known, nothing on earth would have prevented some of them, in their consternation, from effecting an escape. As it was, only Curtis, Falsten, and myself were cognizant of the terrible secret.

As soon as order was restored, the mate and, I joined Falsten on the poop, where he had remained throughout the panic, and where we found him with folded arms, deep in thought, as it might be, solving some hard mechanical problem. He promised, at my request, that he would reveal nothing of the new danger to which we were exposed through Ruby's imprudence. Curtis himself took the responsibility of informing Captain Huntly of our critical situation.

In order to insure complete secrecy, it was necessary to secure the person of the unhappy Ruby, who, quite beside himself, continued to rave up and down the deck with the incessant cry of "Fire! fire!" Accordingly Curtis gave orders to some of his men to seize him and gag him; and before he could make any resistance the miserable man was captured and safely lodged in confinement in his own cabin.

CHAPTER XII.

OCTOBER 22nd.—Curtis has told the captain everything; for he persists in ostensibly recognizing him as his superior officer, and refuses to conceal from him our true situation. Captain Huntly received the communication in perfect silence, and merely passing his hand across his forehead as though to, banish some distressing thought, re-entered his cabin without a word.

Curtis, Lieutenant Walter, Falsten, and myself have been discussing the chances of our safety, and I am surprised to find with how much composure we can all survey our anxious predicament.

"There is no doubt" said Curtis, "that we must abandon all hope of arresting the fire; the heat towards the bow has already become well-nigh unbearable, and the time must come when the flames will find a vent through the deck. If the sea is calm enough for us to make use of the boats, well and good; we shall of course get quit of the ship as quietly as we can; if on the other hand, the weather should be adverse, or the wind be boisterous, we must stick to our place, and contend with the flames to the very last; perhaps, after all, we shall fare better with the fire as a declared enemy than as a hidden one."

Falsten and I agreed with what he said, but I pointed out to him that he had quite overlooked the fact of there being thirty pounds of combustible matter in the hold.

"No" he gravely replied, "I have not forgotten it, but it is a circumstance of which I do not trust myself to think I dare not run the risk of admitting air into the hold by going down to search for the powder, and yet I know not at what moment it may explode. No; it is a matter that I cannot take at all into my reckoning, it must remain in higher hands than mine."

We bowed our heads in a silence which was solemn. In the present state of the weather, immediate flight was, we knew, impossible.

After a considerable pause, Falsten, as calmly as though he were delivering some philosophic dogma, observed,—

"The explosion, if I may use the formula of science, is not necessary, but contingent."

"But tell me, Mr. Falsten," I asked, "is it possible for picrate of potash to ignite without concussion?"

"Certainly it is," replied the engineer. "Under-ordinary circumstances, picrate of potash although not MORE inflammable than common powder, yet possesses the same degree of inflammability."

We now prepared to go on deck. As we left the saloon, in which we had been sitting, Curtis seized my hand.

"Oh, Mr. Kazallon," he exclaimed, "if you only knew the bitterness of the agony I feel at seeing this fine vessel doomed to be devoured by flames, and at being so powerless to save her." Then quickly recovering himself, he continued, "But I am forgetting myself; you, if no other, must know what I am suffering. It is all over now," he said more cheerfully.

"Is our condition quite desperate?" I asked.

"It is just this," he answered deliberately "we are over a mine, and already the match has been applied to the train. How long that train may be, 'tis not for me to say." And with these words he left me.

The other passengers, in common with the crew, are still in entire ignorance of the extremity of peril to which we are exposed, although they are all aware that there is fire in the hold. As soon as the fact was announced, Mr. Kear, after communicating to Curtis his instructions that he thought he should have the fire immediately extinguished and intimating that he held him responsible for all contingencies that might happen, retired to his cabin, where he has remained ever since, fully occupied in collecting and packing together the more cherished articles of his property and without the semblance of a care or a thought for his unfortunate wife, whose condition, in spite of her ludicrous complaints, was truly pitiable. Miss Herbey, however, is unrelaxing in her attentions, and the unremitted diligence with which she fulfills her offices of duty, commands my highest admiration.

OCTOBER 23rd.—This morning, Captain Huntly sent for Curtis into his cabin, and the mate has since made me acquainted with what passed between them.

"Curtis," began the captain, his haggard eye betraying only too plainly some mental derangement, "I am a sailor, am I not?"

"Certainly, captain," was the prompt acquiescence of the mate.

"I do not know how it is," continued the captain, "but I seem bewildered; I cannot recollect anything. Are we not bound for Liverpool? Ah! yes! of course. And have we kept a north-easterly direction since we left?"

"No, sir, according to your orders we have been sailing south-east, and here we are in the tropics."

"And what is the name of the ship?"

"The 'Chancellor,' sir."

"Yes, yes, the 'Chancellor,' so it is. Well, Curtis, I really can't take her back to the north. I hate the sea, the very sight of it makes me ill, I would much rather not leave my cabin."

Curtis went on to tell me how he had tried to persuade him that with a little time and care he would soon recover his indisposition, and feel himself again; but the captain had interrupted him by saying,—

"Well, well; we shall see by-and-by; but for the present you must take this for my positive order; you must, from this time, at once take the command of the ship, and act just as if I were not on board. Under present circumstances, I can do nothing. My brain is all in a whirl, you cannot tell what I am suffering;" and the unfortunate man pressed both his hands convulsively against his forehead.

"I weighed the matter carefully for a moment," added Curtis, "and seeing what his condition too truly was, I acquiesced in all that he required and withdrew, promising him that all his orders should be obeyed."

After hearing these particulars, I could not help remarking how fortunate it was that the captain had resigned of his own accord, for although he might not be actually insane, it was very evident that his brain was in a very morbid condition.

"I succeed him at a very critical moment;" said Curtis thoughtfully; "but I shall endeavour to do my duty."

A short time afterwards he sent for the boatswain, and ordered him to assemble the crew at the foot of the main-mast. As soon as the men were together, he addressed them very calmly, but very firmly.

"My men," he said, "I have to tell you that Captain Huntly, on account of the dangerous situation in which circumstances have placed us, and for other reasons known to myself, has thought right to resign his command to me. From this time forward, I am captain of this vessel."

Thus quietly and simply the change was effected, and we have the satisfaction of knowing that the "Chancellor" is now under the command of a conscientious, energetic man, who will shirk nothing that he believes to be for our common good. M. Letourneur, Andre, Mr. Falsten, and myself immediately offered him our best wishes, in which Lieutenant Walter and the boatswain most cordially joined.

The ship still holds her course south-west and Curtis crowds on all sail and makes as speedily as possible for the nearest of the Lesser Antilles.

CHAPTER XIII.

OCTOBER 24th to 29th.—For the last five days the sea has been very heavy, and although the "Chancellor" sails with wind and wave in her favour, yet her progress is considerably impeded. Here on board this veritable fireship I cannot help contemplating with a longing eye this vast ocean that surrounds us. The water supply should be all we need.

"Why not bore the deck?" I said to Curtis. "Why not admit the water by tons into the hold? What could be the harm? The fire would be quenched; and what would be easier than to pump the water out again?"

"I have already told you, Mr. Kazallon," said Curtis, "that the very moment we admit the air, the flames will rush forth to the very top of the masts. No; we must have courage and patience; we must wait. There is nothing whatever to be done, except to close every aperture."

The fire continued to progress even more rapidly than we had hitherto suspected. The heat gradually drove the passengers nearly all, on deck, and the two stern cabins, lighted, as I said, by their windows in the aft-board were the only quarters below that were inhabitable. Of these Mrs. Kear occupied one, and Curtis reserved the other for Ruby, who, a raving maniac, had to be kept rigidly under restraint. I went down occasionally to see him, but invariably found him in a state of abject terror, uttering horrible shrieks, as though possessed with the idea that he was being scorched by the most excruciating heat.

Once or twice, too, I looked in upon the ex-captain. He was always calm and spoke quite rationally upon any subject except his own profession; but in connexion with that he prated away the merest nonsense. He suffered greatly, but steadily declined all my offers of attention, and pertinaciously refused to leave his cabin.

To-day, an acrid, nauseating smoke made its way through the panellings that partition off the quarters of the crew. At once Curtis ordered the partition to be enveloped in wet tarpaulin, but the fumes penetrated even this, and filled the whole neighbourhood of the ship's bows with a reeking vapour that was positively stifling. As we listened, too, we could hear a dull rumbling sound, but we were as mystified as ever to comprehend where the air could have entered that was evidently fanning the flames. Only too certainly, it was now becoming a question not of days nor even of hours before we must be prepared for the final catastrophe. The sea was still running high, and escape by the boats was plainly impossible. Fortunately, as I have said, the main-mast and the mizzen are of iron; otherwise the heat at their base would long ago have brought them down and our chances of safety would have been much imperiled; but by crowding on sail the "Chancellor" in the full north-east wind continued to make her way with undiminished speed.

It is now a fortnight since the fire was first discovered, and the proper working of the ship has gradually become a more and more difficult matter. Even with thick shoes any attempt to walk upon deck up to the forecastle was soon impracticable, and the poop, simply because its door is elevated somewhat above the level of the hold, is now the only available standing-place. Water began to lose its effect upon the scorched and shrivelling planks; the resin oozed out from the knots in the wood, the seams burst open, and the tar, melted by the heat, followed the rollings of the vessel, and formed fantastic patterns about the deck.

Then to complete our perplexity, the wind shifted suddenly round to the north-west, whence it blew a perfect hurricane. To no purpose did Curtis do everything in his power to bring the ship ahull; every effort was vain; the "Chancellor" could not bear her trysail, so there was nothing to be done but to let her go with the wind, and drift further and further from the land for which we are longing so eagerly.

To-day, the 29th, the tempest seemed to reach its height; the waves appeared to us mountains high, and dashed the spray most violently across the deck. A boat could not live for a moment in such a sea.

Our situation is terrible. We all wait in silence, some few on the forecastle, the great proportion of us on the poop. As for the picrate, for the time we have quite forgotten its existence; indeed it might almost seem as though its explosion would come as a relief, for no catastrophe, however terrible, could far exceed the torture of our suspense.

While he had still the remaining chance, Curtis rescued from the store-room such few provisions as the heat of the compartment allowed him to obtain; and a lot of cases of salt meat and biscuits, a cask of brandy, some barrels of fresh water, together with some sails and wraps, a compass and other instruments are now lying packed in a mass all ready for prompt removal to the boats whenever we shall be obliged to leave the ship.

About eight o'clock in the evening, a noise is heard, distinct even above the raging of the hurricane. The panels of the deck are upheaved, and volumes of black smoke issue upwards as if from a safety-valve. An universal consternation seizes one and all: we must leave the volcano which is about to burst beneath our feet. The crew run to Curtis for orders. He hesitates; looks first at the huge and threatening waves; looks then at the boats. The long-boat is there, suspended right along the centre of the deck;

but it is impossible to approach it now; the yawl, however, hoisted on the starboard side, and the whale-boat suspended aft, are still available. The sailors make frantically for the yawl.

"Stop, stop," shouts Curtis; "do you mean to cut off our last and only chance of safety? Would you launch a boat in such a sea as this?"

A few of them, with Owen at their head, give no heed to what he says. Rushing to the poop, and seizing a cutlass, Curtis shouts again,—

"Touch the tackling of the davit, one of you; only touch it, and I'll cleave your skull."

Awed by his determined manner, the men retire, some clambering into the shrouds, whilst others mount to the very top of the masts.

At eleven o'clock, several loud reports are heard, caused by the bursting asunder of the partitions of the hold. Clouds of smoke issue from the front, followed by a long tongue of lambent flame that seems to encircle the mizzen-mast. The fire now reaches to the cabin occupied by Mrs. Kear, who, shrieking wildly, is brought on deck by Miss Herbey. A moment more, and Silas Huntly makes his appearance, his face all blackened with the grimy smoke; he bows to Curtis, as he passes, and then proceeds in the calmest manner to mount the aft-shrouds, and installs himself at the very top of the mizzen.

The sight of Huntly recalls to my recollection the prisoner still below, and my first impulse is to rush to the staircase and do what I can to set him free. But the maniac has already eluded his confinement, and with singed hair and his clothes already alight, rushes upon deck. Like a salamander he passes across the burning deck with unscathed feet, and glides through the stifling smoke with unchoked breath. Not a sound escapes his lips.

Another loud report; the long-boat is shivered into fragments; the middle panel bursts the tarpaulin that covered it, and a stream of fire, free at length from the restraint that had held it, rises half-mast high.

"The picrate! the picrate!" shrieks the madman; "we shall all be blown up! the picrate will blow us all up."

And in an instant, before we can get near him, he has hurled himself, through the open hatchway, down into the fiery furnace below.

CHAPTER XIV.

OCTOBER 29th:—NIGHT.—The scene, as night came on, was terrible indeed. Notwithstanding the desperateness of our situation, however, there was not one of us so paralyzed by fear, but that we fully realized the horror of it all.

Poor Ruby, indeed, is lost and gone, but his last words were productive of serious consequences. The sailors caught his cry of "Picrate, picrate!" and being thus for the first time made aware of the true nature of their peril, they resolved at every hazard to accomplish their escape. Beside themselves with terror, they either did not or would not, see that no boat could brave the tremendous waves that were raging around, and accordingly they made a frantic rush towards the yawl. Curtis again made a vigorous endeavour to prevent them, but this time all in vain; Owen urged them on, and already the tackling was loosened, so that the boat was swung over to the ship's side, For a moment it hung suspended in mid-air, and then, with a final effort from the sailors, it was quickly lowered into the sea. But scarcely had it touched the water, when it was caught by an enormous wave which, recoiling with resistless violence, dashed it to atoms against the "Chancellor's" side.

The men stood aghast; they were dumbfoundered. Long-boat and yawl both gone, there was nothing now remaining to us but a small whale-boat. Not a word was spoken; not a sound was heard but the hoarse whistling of the wind, and the mournful roaring of the flames. From the centre of the ship, which was hollowed out like a furnace, there issued a column of sooty vapour that ascended to the sky. All the passengers, and several of the crew, took refuge in the aft-quarters of the poop. Mrs. Kear was lying senseless on one of the hen-coops, with Miss Herbey sitting passively at her side; M. Letourneur held his son tightly clasped to his bosom. I saw Falsten calmly consult his watch, and note down the time in his memorandum-book, but I was far from sharing his, composure, for I was overcome by a nervous agitation that I could not suppress.

As far as we knew, Lieutenant Walter, the boatswain, and such of the crew as were not with us, were safe in the bow; but it was impossible to tell how they were faring because the sheet of fire intervened like a curtain, and cut off all communication between stem and stern.

I broke the dismal silence, saying "All over now, Curtis."

"No, sir, not yet," he replied, "now that the panel is open we will set to work, and pour water with all our might down into the furnace, and may be, we shall put it out, even yet."

"But how can you work your pumps while the deck is burning? and how can you get at your men beyond that sheet of flame?"

He made no answer to my impetuous questions, and finding that he had nothing more to say, I repeated that it was all over now.

After a pause, he said, "As long as a plank of the ship remains to stand on, Mr. Kazallon, I shall not give up my hope."

But the conflagration raged with redoubled fury, the sea around us was lighted with a crimson glow, and the clouds above shone with a lurid glare. Long jets of fire darted across the hatchways, and we were forced to take refuge on the taffrail at the extreme end of the poop. Mrs. Kear was laid in the whale-boat that hung from the stern, Miss Herbey persisting to the last in retaining her post by her side.

No pen could adequately portray the horrors of this fearful night. The "Chancellor" under bare poles, was driven, like a gigantic fire-ship with frightful velocity across the raging ocean; her very speed as it were, making common cause with the hurricane to fan the fire that was consuming her. Soon there could be no alternative between throwing ourselves into the sea, or perishing in the flames.

But where, all this time, was the picrate? perhaps, after all, Ruby had deceived us and there was no volcano, such as we dreaded, below our feet.

At half-past eleven, when the tempest seems at its very height there is heard a peculiar roar distinguishable even above the crash of the elements. The sailors in an instant recognize its import.

"Breakers to starboard!" is the cry.

Curtis leaps on to the netting, casts a rapid glance at the snow-white billows, and turning to the helmsman shouts with all his might "Starboard the helm!"

But it is too late. There is a sudden shock; the ship is caught up by an enormous wave; she rises upon her beam ends; several times she strikes the ground; the mizzen-mast snaps short off level with the deck, falls into the sea, and the "Chancellor" is motionless.

CHAPTER XV.

THE NIGHT OF THE 29th CONTINUED.—It was not yet midnight; the darkness was most profound, and we could see nothing. But was it probable that we had stranded on the coast of America?

Very shortly after the ship had thus come to a standstill a clanking of chains was heard proceeding from her bows.

"That is well," said Curtis; "Walter and the boatswain have cast both the anchors. Let us hope they will hold."

Then, clinging to the netting, he clambered along the starboard side, on which the ship had heeled, as far as the flames would allow him. He clung to the holdfasts of the shrouds, and in spite of the heavy seas that dashed against the vessel he maintained his position for a considerable time, evidently listening to some sound that had caught his ear in the midst of the tempest. In about a quarter of an hour he returned to the poop.

"Heaven be praised!" he said, "the water is coming in, and perhaps may get the better of the fire."

"True," said I, "but what then?"

"That," he replied, "is a question for by-and-by. We can now only think of the present."

Already I fancied that the violence of the flames was somewhat abated, and that the two opposing elements were in fierce contention. Some plank in the ship's side was evidently stove in, admitting free passage for the waves. But how, when the water had mastered the fire, should we be able to master the water? Our natural course would be to use the pumps, but these, in the very midst of the conflagration, were quite unavailable.

For three long hours, in anxious suspense, we watched and watched, and waited. Where we were we could not tell. One thing alone was certain: the tide was ebbing beneath us, and the waves were relaxing in their violence. Once let the fire be extinguished, and then, perhaps, there would be room to hope that the next high tide would set us afloat.

Towards half-past four in the morning the curtain of fire and smoke, which had shut off communication between the two extremities of the ship, became less dense, and we could faintly distinguish that party of the crew who had taken refuge in the forecastle; and before long, although it was impracticable to step upon the deck, the lieutenant and the boatswain contrived to clamber over the gunwale, along the rails, and joined Curtis on the poop.

Here they held a consultation, to which I was admitted. They were all of opinion that nothing could be done until daylight should give us something of an idea of our actual position. If we then found that we were near the shore, we would, weather permitting, endeavour to land, either in the boat or upon a raft. If, on the other hand, no land were in sight, and the "Chancellor" were ascertained to be stranded on some isolated reef, all we could do would be to get her afloat, and put her into condition for reaching the nearest coast. Curtis told us that it was long since he had been able to take any observation of altitude, but there was no doubt the north-west wind had driven us far to the south; and he thought, as he was ignorant of the existence of any reef in this part of the Atlantic, that it was just possible that we had been driven on to the coast of some portion of South America.

I reminded him that we were in momentary expectation of an explosion, and suggested that it would be advisable to abandon the ship and take refuge on the reef. But he would not hear of such a proceeding, said that the reef would probably be covered at high tide, and persisted in the original resolution, that no decided action could be taken before the daylight appeared.

I immediately reported this decision of the captain to my fellow passengers. None of them seem to realize the new danger to which the "Chancellor" may be exposed by being cast upon an unknown reef, hundreds of miles it may be from land. All are for the time possessed with one idea, one hope; and that is, that the fire may now be quenched and the explosion averted.

And certainly their hopes seem in a fair way of being fulfilled. Already the raging flames that poured forth from the hatches have given place to dense black smoke, and although occasionally some fiery streaks dart across the dusky fumes, yet they are instantly extinguished. The waves are doing what pumps and buckets could never have effected; by their inundation they are steadily stifling the fire which was as steadily spreading to the whole bulk of the 1700 bales of cotton.

CHAPTER XVI.

OCTOBER 30th.—At the first gleam of daylight we eagerly scanned the southern and western horizons, but the morning mists limited our view. Land was nowhere to be seen. The tide was now almost at its lowest ebb, and the colour of the few peaks of rock that jutted up around us showed that the reef on which we had stranded was of basaltic formation. There were now only about six feet of water around the "Chancellor," though with a full freight she draws about fifteen. It was remarkable how far she had been carried on to the shelf of rock, but the number of times that she had touched the bottom before she finally ran aground left us no doubt that she had been lifted up and borne along on the top of an enormous wave. She now lies with her stern considerably higher than her bows, a position which renders walking upon the deck anything but an easy matter; moreover as the tide-receded she heeled over so much to larboard that at one time Curtis feared she would altogether capsize; that fear, however, since the tide has reached its lowest mark, has happily proved groundless.

At six o'clock some violent blows were felt against the ship's side, and at the same time a voice was distinguished, shouting loudly, "Curtis! Curtis!" Following the direction of the cries we saw that the broken mizzen-mast was being washed against the vessel, and in the dusky morning twilight we could make out the figure of a man clinging to the rigging. Curtis, at the peril of his life, hastened to bring the man on board, It proved to be none other than Silas Huntly, who, after being carried overboard with the mast, had thus, almost by a miracle, escaped a watery grave. Without a word of thanks to his deliverer, the ex-captain, passive, like an automaton, passed on and took his seat in the most secluded corner of the poop. The broken mizzen may, perhaps, be of service to us at some future time, and with that idea it has been rescued from the waves and lashed securely to the stern.

By this time it was light enough to see for a distance of three miles round; but as yet nothing could be discerned to make us think that we were near a coast. The line of breakers ran for about a mile from south-west to north-east, and two hundred fathoms to the north of the ship an irregular mass of rocks formed a small islet. This islet rose about fifty feet above the sea, and was consequently above the level of the highest tides; whilst a sort of causeway, available at low water, would enable us to reach the island, if necessity required. But there the reef ended; beyond it the sea again resumed its sombre hue, betokening deep water. In all probability, then, this was a solitary shoal, unattached to a shore, and the gloom of a bitter disappointment began to weigh upon our spirits.

In another hour the mists had totally disappeared, and it was broad daylight. I and M. Letourneur stood watching Curtis as he continued eagerly to scan the western horizon. Astonishment was written on his countenance; to him it appeared perfectly incredible that, after our course for so long had been due south from the Bermudas, no land should be in sight. But not a speck, however minute, broke the clearly-defined line that joined sea and sky. After a time Curtis made his way along the netting to the shrouds, and swung himself quickly up to the top of the mainmast. For several minutes he remained there examining the open space around, then seizing one of the backstays he glided down and rejoined us on the poop.

"No land in sight," he said, in answer to our eager looks of inquiry.

At this point Mr. Kear interposed, and in a gruff, ill-tempered tone, asked Curtis where we were. Curtis replied that he did not know.

"You don't know, sir? Then all I can say is that you ought to know!" exclaimed the petroleum merchant.

"That may be, sir; but at present I am as ignorant of our whereabouts as you are yourself," said Curtis.

"Well," said Mr. Kear, "just please to know that I don't want to stay for ever on your everlasting ship, so I beg you will make haste and start off again."

Curtis condescended to make no other reply than a shrug of the shoulders, and turning away he informed M. Letourneur and myself that if the sun came out he intended to take its altitude and find out to what part of the ocean we had been driven. His next care was to distribute preserved meat and biscuit amongst the passengers and crew already half fainting with hunger and fatigue, and then he set to work to devise measures for setting the ship afloat.

The conflagration was greatly abated; no flames now appeared, and although some black smoke still issued from the interior, yet its volume was far less than before. The first step was to discover how much water had entered the hold. The deck was still too hot to walk upon; but after two hours' irrigation the boards became sufficiently cool for the boatswain to proceed to take some soundings, and he shortly afterwards announced that there were five feet of water below. This the captain determined should not be pumped out at present, as he wanted it thoroughly to do its duty before he got rid of it.

The next subject for consideration was whether it would be advisable to abandon the vessel, and to take refuge on the reef. Curtis thought not; and the lieutenant and the boatswain agreed with him. The chances of an explosion were greatly diminished, as it had been ascertained that the water had reached that part of the hold in which Ruby's luggage had been deposited; while, on the other hand, in the event of rough weather, our position even upon the most elevated points of rock might be very critical. It was accordingly resolved that both passengers and crew were safest on board.

Acting upon this decision we proceeded to make a kind of encampment on the poop, and the few mattresses that were rescued uninjured have been given up for the use of the two ladies. Such of the crew as had saved their hammocks have been told to place them under the forecastle where they would have to stow themselves as best they could, their ordinary quarters being absolutely uninhabitable.

Fortunately, although the store-room has been considerably exposed to the heat, its contents are not very seriously damaged, and all the barrels of water and the greater part of the provisions are quite intact. The stack of spare sails, which had been packed away in front, is also free from injury. The wind has dropped considerably since the early morning, and the swell in the sea is far less heavy. On the whole our spirits are reviving, and we begin to think we may yet find a way out of our troubles.

M. Letourneur, his son, and I, have just had a long conversation about the ship's officers. We consider their conduct, under the late trying circumstances, to have been most exemplary, and their courage, energy, and endurance to have been beyond all praise. Lieutenant Walter, the boatswain, and Dowlas the carpenter have all alike distinguished themselves, and made us feel that they are men to be relied on. As for Curtis, words can scarcely be found to express our admiration of his character; he is the same as he has ever been, the very life of his crew, cheering them on by word or gesture; finding an expedient for every difficulty, and always foremost in every action.

The tide turned at seven this morning, and by eleven all the rocks were submerged, none of them being visible except the cluster of those which formed the rim of a small and almost circular basin from 250 to 300 feet in diameter, in the north angle of which the ship is lying. As the tide rose the white breakers disappeared, and the sea, fortunately for the "Chancellor," was pretty calm; otherwise the dashing of the waves against her sides, as she lies motionless, might have been attended by serious consequences.

As might be supposed, the height of the water in the hold increased with the tide from five feet to nine; but this was rather a matter for congratulation, inasmuch as it sufficed to inundate another layer of cotton.

At half-past eleven the sun, which had been behind the clouds since ten o'clock, broke forth brightly. The captain, who had already in the morning been able to calculate an horary angle, now prepared to take the meridian altitude, and succeeded at midday in making his observation most satisfactorily. After retiring for a short time to calculate the result; he returned to the poop and announced that we are in lat; 18deg. 5min. N. and long. 45deg. 53min. W., but that the reef on which we are aground is not marked upon the charts. The only explanation that can be given for the omission is that the islet must be of recent formation, and has been caused by some subterranean volcanic disturbance. But whatever may be the solution of the mystery, here we are 800 miles from land; for such, on consulting the map, we find to be the actual distance to the coast of Guiana, which is the nearest shore. Such is the position to which we have been brought, in the first place, by Huntly's senseless obstinacy, and, secondly, by the furious north-west gale.

Yet, after all, the captain's communication does not dishearten us. As I said before, our spirits are reviving. We have escaped the peril of fire; the fear of explosion is past and gone; and oblivious of the fact that the ship with a hold full of water is only too likely to founder when she puts out to sea, we feel a confidence in the future that forbids us to despond.

Meanwhile Curtis prepares to do all that common sense demands. He proposes, when the fire is quite extinguished, to throw overboard the whole, or the greater portion of the cargo, including of course, the picrate; he will next plug up the leak, and then, with a lightened ship, he will take advantage of the first high tide to quit the reef as speedily as possible.

CHAPTER XVII.

OCTOBER 30th.—Once again I talked to M. Letourneur about our situation, and endeavoured to animate him with the hope that we should not be detained for long in our present predicament; but he could not be brought to take a very sanguine view of our prospects.

"But surely," I protested, "it will not be difficult to throw overboard a few hundred bales of cotton; two or three days at most will suffice for that."

"Likely enough," he replied, "when the business is once begun; but you must remember, Mr. Kazallon, that the very heart of the cargo is still smouldering, and that it will still be several days before any one will be able to venture into the hold. Then the leak, too, that has to be caulked; and, unless it is stopped up very effectually, we shall be only doomed most certainly to perish at sea. Don't, then, be deceiving yourself; it must be three weeks at least before you can expect to put out to sea. I can only hope meanwhile that the weather will continue propitious; it wouldn't take many storms to knock the 'Chancellor,' shattered as she is, completely into pieces."

Here, then, was the suggestion of a new danger to which we were to be exposed; the fire might be extinguished, the water might be got rid of by the pumps, but, after all, we must be at the mercy of the wind and waves; and, although the rocky island might afford a temporary refuge from the tempest, what was to become of passengers and crew if the vessel should be reduced to a total wreck? I made no remonstrance, however, to this view of our case, but merely asked M. Letourneur if he had confidence in Robert Curtis?

"Perfect confidence," he answered; "and I acknowledge it most gratefully, as a providential circumstance, that Captain Huntly had given him the command in time. Whatever man can do I know that Curtis will not leave undone to extricate us from our dilemma."

Prompted by this conversation with M. Letourneur I took the first opportunity of trying to ascertain from Curtis himself, how long he reckoned we should be obliged to remain upon the reef; but he merely replied, that it must depend upon circumstances, and that he hoped the weather would continue favourable. Fortunately the barometer is rising steadily, and there is every sign of a prolonged calm.

Meantime Curtis is taking active measures for totally extinguishing the fire. He is at no great pains to spare the cargo, and as the bales that lie just above the level of the water are still a-light he has resorted to the expedient of thoroughly saturating the upper layers of the cotton, in order that the combustion may be stifled between the moisture descending from above and that ascending from below. This scheme has brought the pumps once more into requisition. At present the crew are adequate to the task of working them, but I and some of our fellow passengers are ready to offer our assistance whenever it shall be necessary.

With no immediate demand upon our labour, we are thrown upon our own resources for passing our time. Letourneur, Andre and myself, have frequent conversations; I also devote an hour or two to my diary. Falsten holds little communication with any of us, but remains absorbed in his calculations, and amuses himself by tracing mechanical diagrams with ground-plan, section, elevation, all complete. It would be a happy inspiration if he could invent some mighty engine that could set us all afloat again. Mr. and Mrs. Kear, too, hold themselves aloof from their fellow passengers, and we are not sorry to be relieved from the necessity of listening to their incessant grumbling; unfortunately, however, they carry off Miss Herbey with them, so that we enjoy little or nothing of the young lady's society. As for Silas Huntly, he has become a complete nonentity; he exists, it is true, but merely, it would seem, to vegetate.

Hobart, the steward, an obsequious, sly sort of fellow, goes through his routine of duties just as though the vessel were pursuing her ordinary course; and, as usual, is continually falling out with Jynxstrop, the cook, an impudent, ill-favoured negro, who interferes with the other sailors in a manner which, I think, ought not to be allowed.

Since it appears likely that we shall have abundance of time on our hands, I have proposed to M. Letourneur and his son that we shall together explore the reef on which we are stranded. It is not very probable that we shall be able to discover much about the origin of this strange accumulation of rock, yet the attempt will at least occupy us for some hours, and will relieve us from the monotony of our confinement on board. Besides, as the reef is not marked in any of the maps, I could not but believe that it would be rendering a service to hydrography if we were to take an accurate plan of the rocks, of which Curtis could afterwards verify the true position by a second observation made with a closer precision than the one he has already taken.

M. Letourneur agrees to my proposal, Curtis has promised to let us have the boat and some sounding-lines, and to allow one of the sailors to accompany us; so to-morrow morning, we hope to make our little voyage of investigation.

CHAPTER XVIII.

OCTOBER 31st to NOVEMBER 5th.—Our first proceeding on the morning of the 31st was to make the proposed tour of the reef, which is about a quarter of a mile long. With the aid of our sounding-lines we found that the water was deep, right up to the very rocks, and that no shelving shores prevented us coasting along them. There was not a shadow of doubt as to the rock being of purely volcanic origin, upheaved by some mighty subterranean convulsion. It is formed of blocks of basalt, arranged in perfect order, of which the regular prisms give the whole mass the effect of being one gigantic crystal; and the remarkable transparency of the sea enabled us plainly to observe the curious shafts of the prismatic columns that support the marvelous substructure.

"This is indeed a singular island," said M. Letourneur; "evidently it is of quite a recent origin."

"Yes, father," said Andre, "and I should think it has been caused by a phenomenon similar to those which produced the Julia Island, off the coast of Sicily, or the group of the Santorini, in the Grecian Archipelago. One could almost fancy that it had been created expressly for the 'Chancellor' to stand upon."

"It is very certain," I observed, "that some upheaving has lately taken place. This is by no means an unfrequented part of the Atlantic, so that it is not at all likely that it could have escaped the notice of sailors if it had been always in existence; yet it is not marked even in the most modern charts. We must try and explore it thoroughly and give future navigators the benefit of our observations."

"But, perhaps, it will disappear as it came," said Andre. "You are no doubt aware, Mr. Kazallon, that these volcanic islands sometimes have a very transitory existence. Not impossibly, by the time it gets marked upon the maps it may no longer be here."

"Never mind, my boy," answered his father, "it is better to give warning of a danger that does not exist than overlook one that does. I daresay the sailors will not grumble much, if they don't find a reef where we have marked one."

"No, I daresay not, father," said Andre "and after all this island is very likely as firm as a continent. However, if it is to disappear, I expect Captain Curtis would be glad to see it take its departure as soon as possible after he has finished his repairs; it would save him a world of trouble in getting his ship afloat."

"Why, what a fellow you are Andre!" I said, laughing, "I believe you would like to rule Nature with a magic wand; first of all, you would call up a reef from the depth of the ocean to give the 'Chancellor' time to extinguish her flames, and then you would make it disappear just that the ship might be free again."

Andre smiled; then, in a more serious tone, he expressed his gratitude for the timely help that had been vouchsafed us in our hour of need.

The more we examined the rocks that formed the base of the little island, the more we became convinced that its formation was quite recent, Not a mollusk, not a tuft of seaweed was found clinging to the sides of the rocks; not a germ had the wind carried to its surface, not a bird had taken refuge amidst the crags upon its summits. To a lover of natural history, the spot did not yield a single point of interest; the geologist alone would find subject of study in the basaltic mass.

When we reached the southern point of the island I proposed that we should disembark. My companions readily assented, young Letourneur jocosely observing that if the little island was destined to vanish, it was quite right that it should first be visited by human beings. The boat was accordingly brought alongside, and we set, foot upon the reef, and began to ascend the gradual slope that leads to its highest elevation.

The walking was not very rough, and as Andre could get along tolerably well without the assistance of an arm, he led the way, his father and I following close behind. A quarter of an hour sufficed to bring us to the loftiest point in the islet, when we seated ourselves on the basaltic prism that crowned its summit.

Andre took a sketch-book from his pocket, and proceeded to make a drawing of the reef. Scarcely had he completed the outline when his father exclaimed,—

"Why, Andre, you have drawn a ham!"

"Something uncommonly like it, I confess," replied Andre. "I think we had better ask Captain Curtis to let us call our island Ham Rock."

"Good," said I; "though sailors will need to keep it at a respectful distance, for they will scarcely find that their teeth are strong enough to tackle with it."

M. Letourneur was quite correct; the outline of the reef as it stood clearly defined against the deep green water resembled nothing so much, as a fine

York ham, of which the little creek, where the "Chancellor" had been stranded, corresponded to the hollow place above the knuckle. The tide at this time was low, and the ship now lay heeled over very much to the starboard side, the few points of rock that emerged in the extreme south of the reef plainly marking the narrow passage through which she had been forced before she finally ran aground.

As soon as Andre had finished his sketch we descended by a slope as gradual as that by which we had come up, and made our way towards the west. We had not gone very far when a beautiful grotto, perfect as an architectural structure, arrested our attention, M. Letourneur and Andre who have visited the Hebrides, pronounced it to be a Fingal's cave in miniature; a Gothic chapel that might form a fit vestibule for the cathedral cave of Staffa. The basaltic rocks had cooled down into the same regular concentric prisms; there was the same dark canopied roof with its interstices filled up with its yellow lutings; the same precision of outline in the prismatic angles, sharp as though chiselled by a sculptor's hand; the same sonorous vibration of the air across the basaltic rocks, of which the Gaelic poets have feigned that the harps of the Fingal minstrelsy were made. But whereas at Staffa the floor of the cave is always covered with a sheet of water, here the grotto was beyond the reach of all but the highest waves, whilst the prismatic shafts themselves formed quite a solid pavement.

After remaining nearly an hour in our newly-discovered grotto we returned to the "Chancellor," and communicated the result of our explorations to Curtis, who entered the island upon his chart by the name that Andre Letourneur had proposed.

Since its discovery we have not permitted a day to pass without spending some time in our Ham Rock grotto. Curtis has taken an opportunity of visiting it, but he is too preoccupied with other matters to have much interest to spare for the wonders of nature. Falsten, too, came once and examined the character of the rocks, knocking and chipping them about with all the mercilessness of a geologist. Mr. Kear would not trouble himself to leave the ship; and although I asked his wife to join us in one of our excursions she declined, upon the plea that the fatigue, as well as the inconvenience of embarking in the boat, would be more than she could bear.

Miss Herbey, only too thankful to escape even for an hour from her capricious mistress, eagerly accepted M. Letourneur's invitation to pay a visit to the reef but to her great disappointment Mrs. Kear at first refused point-blank to allow her to leave the ship. I felt intensely annoyed, and resolved to intercede in Miss Herbey's favour; and as I had already rendered that self-indulgent lady sundry services which she thought she might probably be glad again to accept, I gained my point, and Miss Herbey has several times been permitted to accompany us across the rocks, where the young girl's delight at her freedom has been a pleasure to behold.

Sometimes we fish along the shore, and, then enjoy a luncheon in the grotto, whilst the basalt columns vibrate like harps to the breeze. This arid reef, little as it is, compared with the cramped limits of the "Chancellor's" deck is like some vast domain; soon there will be scarcely a stone with which we are not familiar, scarcely a portion of its surface which we have not merrily trodden, and I am sure that when the hour of departure arrives we shall leave it with regret.

In the course of conversation, Andre Letourneur one day happened to say that he believed the island of Staffa belonged to the Macdonald family, who let it for the small sum of 12 pounds a year.

"I suppose then," said Miss Herbey, "that we should hardly get more than half-a-crown a year for our pet little island."

"I don't think you would get a penny for it, Miss Herbey; but are you thinking of taking a lease?" I said, laughing.

"Not at present," she said; then added, with a half-suppressed sigh, "and yet it is a place where I have seemed to know what it is to be really happy."

Andre murmured some expression of assent, and we all felt that there was something touching in the words of the orphaned, friendless girl who had found her long-lost sense of happiness on a lonely rock in the Atlantic.

CHAPTER XIX.

NOVEMBER 6th to NOVEMBER 15th.—For the first five days after the "Chancellor" had run aground, there was a dense black smoke continually rising from the hold; but it gradually diminished until the 6th of November, when we might consider that the fire was extinguished. Curtis, nevertheless, deemed it prudent to persevere in working the pumps, which he did until the entire hull of the ship, right up to the deck, had been completely inundated.

The rapidity, however, with which the water, at every retreat of the tide, drained off to the level of the sea, was an indication that the leak must be of considerable magnitude; and such, on investigation, proved to be the case. One of the sailors, named Flaypole, dived one day at low water to examine the extent of the damage, and found that the hole was not much less than four feet square, and was situated thirty feet fore of the helm, and two feet above the rider of the keel; three planks had been stoved in by a sharp point of rock, and it was only a wonder that the violence with which the heavily-laden vessel had been thrown ashore did not result in the smashing in of many parts besides.

As it would be a couple of days or more before the hold would be in a condition for the bales of cotton to be removed for the carpenter to examine the damage from the interior of the ship, Curtis employed the interval in having the broken mizzen-mast repaired. Dowlas the carpenter, with considerable skill, contrived to mortice it into its former stump, and made the junction thoroughly secure by strong iron-belts and bolts. The shrouds, the stays and backstays, were then carefully refitted, some of the sails were changed, and the whole of the running rigging was renewed. Injury, to some extent, had been done to the poop and to the crew's lockers, in the front; but time and labour were all that were wanted to make them good; and with such a will, did every one set to work that it was not long before all the cabins were again available for use.

On the 8th the unlading of the ship commenced. Pulleys and tackling were put over the hatches, and passengers and crew together proceeded to haul up the heavy bales which had been deluged so frequently by water that the cotton was all but spoiled. One by one the sodden bales were placed in the boat to be transported to the reef. After the first layer of cotton had been removed it became necessary to drain off part of the water that filled the hold. For this purpose the leak in the side had somehow or other to be stopped, and this was an operation which was cleverly accomplished by Dowlas and Flaypole, who contrived to dive at low tide and nail a sheet of copper over the entire hole. This, however, of itself would have been utterly inadequate to sustain the pressure that would arise from the action of the pumps; so Curtis ordered that a number of the bales should be piled up inside against the broken planks. The scheme succeeded very well, and as the water got lower and lower in the hold the men were enabled to resume their task of unlading.

Curtis thinks it quite probable that the leaks may be mended from the interior. By far the best way of repairing the damage would be to careen the ship, and to shift the planking, but the appliances are wanting for such an undertaking; moreover, any bad weather which might occur while the ship was on her flank would only too certainly be fatal to her altogether. But the captain has very little doubt that by some device or other he shall manage to patch up the hole in such a way as will insure our reaching land in safety.

After two days' toil the water was entirely reduced and without further difficulty the unlading was completed. All of us, including even Andre Letourneur, have been taking our turn at the pumps, for the work is so extremely fatiguing that the crew require some occasional respite; arms and back soon become strained and weary with the incessant swing of the handles, and I can well understand the dislike which sailors always express to the labour.

One thing there is which is much in our favour; the ship lies on a firm and solid bottom, and we have the satisfaction of knowing that we are not contending with a flood that encroaches faster than it can be resisted. Heaven grant that we may not be called to make like efforts, and to make them hopelessly, for a foundering ship!

CHAPTER XX.

NOVEMBER 15th to 20th.—The examination of the hold has at last been made. Amongst the first things that were found was the case of picrate, perfectly intact; having neither been injured by the water, nor of course reached by the flames. Why it was not at once pitched into the sea I cannot say; but it was merely conveyed to the extremity of the island, and there it remains.

While they were below, Curtis and Dowlas made themselves acquainted with the full extent of the mischief that had been done by the conflagration. They found that the deck and the cross-beams that supported it had been much less injured than they expected, and the thick, heavy planks had only been scorched very superficially. But the action of the fire on the flanks of the ship had been of a much more serious character; a long portion of the inside boarding had been burnt away, and the very ribs of the vessel were considerably damaged; the oakum caulkings had all started away from the butt-ends and seams; so much so that it was little short of a miracle that the whole ship had not long since gaped completely open.

The captain and the carpenter returned to the deck with anxious faces. Curtis lost no time in assembling passengers and crew, and announcing to them the facts of the case.

"My friends," he said, "I am here to tell you that the 'Chancellor' has sustained far greater injuries than we suspected, and that her hull is very seriously damaged. If we had been stranded anywhere else than on a barren reef, that may at any time be overwhelmed by a tempestuous sea I should not have hesitated to take the ship to pieces, and construct a smaller vessel that might have carried us safely to land; but I dare not run the risk of remaining here. We are now 800 miles from the coast of Paramaribo, the nearest portion of Dutch Guiana, and in ten or twelve days, if the weather should be favourable, I believe we could reach the shore. What I now propose to do is to stop the leak by the best means we can command, and make at once for the nearest port."

As no better plan seemed to suggest itself, Curtis's proposal was unanimously accepted Dowlas and his assistants immediately set to work to repair the charred frame-work of the ribs, and to stop the leak; they took care thoroughly to caulk from the outside all the seams that were above low water mark; lower than that they were unable to work, and had to content themselves with such repairs as they could effect in the interior. But after all the pains there is no doubt the "Chancellor" is not fit for a long voyage, and would be condemned as unseaworthy at any port at which we might put in.

To-day, the 20th, Curtis having done all that human power could do to repair his ship, determined to put her to sea.

Ever since the "Chancellor" had been relieved of her cargo, and of the water in her hold, she had been able to float in the little natural basin into which she had been driven. The basin was enclosed on either hand by rocks that remained uncovered even at high water, but was sufficiently wide to allow the vessel to turn quite round at its broadest part, and by means of hawsers fastened on the reef to be brought with her bows towards the south; while, to prevent her being carried back on to the reef, she has been anchored fore and aft.

To all appearance, then, it seemed as though it would be an easy matter to put the "Chancellor" to sea; if the wind were favourable the sails would be hoisted, if otherwise, she would have to be towed through the narrow passage. All seemed simple. But unlooked-for difficulties had yet to be surmounted.

The mouth of the passage is guarded by a kind of ridge of basalt, which at high tide we knew was barely covered with sufficient water to float the "Chancellor," even when entirely unfreighted. To be sure she had been carried over the obstacle once before, but then, as I have already said, she had been caught up by an enormous wave, and might have been said to be LIFTED over the barrier into her present position. Besides, on that ever-memorable night, there had not only been the ordinary spring-tide, but an equinoctial tide, such a one as could not be expected to occur again for many months. Waiting was out of the question; so Curtis determined to run the risk, and to take advantage of the spring-tide, which would occur to-day, to make an attempt to get the ship, lightened as she was, over the bar; after which, he might ballast her sufficiently to sail.

The wind was blowing from the north-west, and consequently right in the direction of the passage. The captain, however, after a consultation, preferred to tow the ship over the ridge, as he considered it was scarcely safe to allow a vessel of doubtful stability at full sail to charge an obstacle that would probably bring her to a dead lock. Before the operation was commenced, Curtis took the precaution of having an anchor ready in the stern, for, in the event of the attempt being unsuccessful, it would be necessary to bring the ship back to her present moorings. Two more anchors were next carried outside the passage, which was not more than two hundred feet in length. The chains were attached to the windlass, the sailors worked away at the handspikes, and at four o'clock in the afternoon the "Chancellor" was in motion.

High tide would be at twenty minutes past four, and at ten minutes before that time the ship had been hauled as far as her sea-range would allow; her keel grazed the ridge, and her progress was arrested. When the lowest part of her stern, however, just cleared the obstruction, Curtis deemed that there was no longer any reason why the mechanical action of the wind should not be brought to bear and contribute its assistance. Without delay, all sails were unfurled and trimmed to the wind. The tide was exactly at its height, passengers and crew together were at the windlass, M. Letourneur, Andre, Falsten, and myself being at the starboard bar. Curtis stood upon the poop, giving his chief attention to the sails; the lieutenant was on the forecastle; the boatswain by the helm. The sea seemed propitiously calm and, as it swelled gently to and fro, lifted the ship several times.

"Now, my boys," said Curtis in his calm clear voice, "all together! Off!"

Round went the windlass; click, click, clanked the chains as link by link they were forced through the hawse-holes.

The breeze freshened, and the masts gave to the pressure of the sails, but round and round we went, keeping time in regular monotony to the sing-song tune hummed by one of the sailors.

We had gained about twenty feet, and were redoubling our efforts when the ship grounded again.

And now no effort would avail; all was in vain; the tide began to turn; and the "Chancellor" would not advance an inch. Was there time to go back? She would inevitably go to pieces if left balanced upon the ridge. In an instant the captain has ordered the sails to be furled, and the anchor dropped from the stern.

One moment of terrible anxiety, and all is well.

The "Chancellor" tacks to stern, and glides back into the basin, which is once more her prison.

"Well, captain," says the boatswain, "what's to be done now?"

"I don't know" said Curtis, "but we shall get across somehow."

CHAPTER XXI.

NOVEMBER 21st to 24th.—There was assuredly no time to be lost before we ought to leave Ham Rock reef. The barometer had been falling ever since the morning, the sea was getting rougher, and there was every symptom that the weather, hitherto so favourable, was on the point of breaking; and in the event of a gale the "Chancellor" must inevitably be dashed to pieces on the rocks.

In the evening, when the tide was quite low, and the rocks uncovered, Curtis, the boatswain, and Dowlas went to examine the ridge which had proved so serious an obstruction, Falsten and I accompanied them. We came to the conclusion that the only way of effecting a passage was by cutting away the rocks with pikes over a surface measuring ten feet by six. An extra depth of nine or ten inches would give a sufficient gauge, and the channel might be accurately marked out by buoys; in this way it was conjectured the ship might be got over the ridge and so reach the deep water beyond.

"But this basalt is as hard as granite," said the boatswain; "besides, we can only get at it at low water, and consequently could only work at it for two hours out of the twenty-four."

"All the more reason why we should begin at once, boatswain," said Curtis.

"But if it is to take us a month, captain, perhaps by that time the ship may be knocked to atoms. Couldn't we manage to blow up the rock? we have got some powder on board."

"Not enough for that;" said the boatswain.

"You have something better than powder," said Falsten.

"What's that?" asked the captain.

"Picrate of potash," was the reply.

And so the explosive substance with which poor Ruby had so grievously imperilled the vessel was now to serve her in good stead, and I now saw what a lucky thing it was that the case had been deposited safely on the reef, instead of being thrown into the sea.

Picric acid is a crystalline bitter product extracted from coal-tar, and forming, in combination with potash, a yellow salt known as picrate of potash. The explosive power of this substance is inferior to that of guncotton or of dynamite, but far greater than that of ordinary gunpowder; one grain of picric powder producing an effect equal to that of thirteen grains of common powder. Picrate is easily ignited by any sharp or violent shock, and some gun-priming which we had in our possession would answer the purpose of setting it alight.

The sailors went off at once for their pikes, and Dowlas and his assistants, under the direction of Falsten, who, as an engineer, understood such matters, proceeded to hollow out a mine wherein to deposit the powder. At first we hoped that everything would be ready for the blasting to take place on the following morning, but when daylight appeared we found that the men, although they had laboured with a will, had only been able to work for an hour at low water and that four tides must ebb before the mine had been sunk to the required depth.

Not until eight o'clock on the morning of the 23rd was the work complete. The hole was bored obliquely in the rock, and was large enough to contain about ten pounds of explosive matter. Just as the picrate was being introduced into the aperture, Falsten interposed:—

"Stop," he said, "I think it will be best to mix the picrate with common powder, as that will allow us to fire the mine with a match instead of the gun-priming which would be necessary to produce a shock. Besides, it is an understood thing that the addition of gunpowder renders picrate far more effective in blasting such rocks as this, as then the violence of the picrate prepares the way for the powder which, slower in its action, will complete the disseverment of the basalt."

Falsten is not a great talker, but what he does say is always very much to the point. His good advice was immediately followed; the two substances were mixed together, and after a match had been introduced the compound was rammed closely into the hole.

Notwithstanding that the "Chancellor" was at a distance from the rocks that insured her from any danger of being injured by the explosion, it was thought advisable that the passengers and crew should take refuge in the grotto at the extremity of the reef, and even Mr. Kear, in spite of his many objections, was forced to leave the ship. Falsten, as soon as he had set fire to the match, joined us in our retreat.

The train was to burn for ten minutes, and at the end of that time the explosion took place; the report, on account of the depth of the mine, being muffled, and much less noisy than we had expected. But the operation had been perfectly successful. Before we reached the ridge we could see that the basalt had been literally reduced to powder, and that a little channel, already being filled by the rising tide, had been cut right through the obstacle. A loud hurrah rang through the air; our prison-doors were opened, and we were prisoners no more!

At high tide the "Chancellor" weighed anchor and floated out into the open sea, but she was not in a condition to sail until she had been ballasted; and for the next twenty-four hours the crew were busily employed in taking up blocks of stone, and such of the bales of cotton as had sustained the least amount of injury.

In the course of the day, M. Letourneur, Andre, Miss Herbey, and I took a farewell walk round the reef, and Andre with artistic skill, carved on the wall of the grotto the word "Chancellor,"—the designation Ham Rock, which we had given to the reef,—and the date of our running aground. Then we bade adieu to the scene of our three week's sojourn, where we had passed days that to some at least of our party will be reckoned as far from being the least happy of their lives.

At high tide this morning, the 24th, with low, top, and gallant sails all set, the "Chancellor" started on her onward way, and two hours later the last peak of Ham Rock had vanished below the horizon.

CHAPTER XXII.

NOVEMBER 24th to DECEMBER 1st.—Here we were then once more at sea, and although on board a ship of which the stability was very questionable, we had hopes, if the wind continued favourable, of reaching the coast of Guiana in the course of a few days.

Our way was south-west and consequently with the wind, and although Curtis would not crowd on all sail lest the extra speed should have a tendency to spring the leak afresh, the "Chancellor" made a progress that was quite satisfactory. Life on board began to fall back into its former routine; the feeling of insecurity and the consciousness that we were merely retracing our path doing much, however, to destroy the animated intercourse that would otherwise go on between passenger and passenger.

The first few days passed without any incident worth recording, then on the 29th, the wind shifted to the north, and it became necessary to brace the yards, trim the sails, and take a starboard tack. This made the ship lurch very much on one side, and as Curtis felt that she was labouring far too heavily, he clued up the top-gallants, prudently reckoning that, under the circumstances, caution was far more important than speed.

The night came on dark and foggy. The breeze freshened considerably, and, unfortunately for us, hailed from the north-west. Although we carried no top-sails at all, the ship seemed to heel over more than ever. Most of the passengers had retired to their cabins, but all the crew remained on deck, whilst Curtis never quitted his post upon the poop.

Towards two o'clock in the morning I was myself preparing to go to my cabin, when Burke, one of the sailors who had been down into the hold, came on deck with the ominous cry,—

"Two feet of water below."

In an instant Curtis and the boatswain had descended the ladder. The startling news was only too true; the sea-water was entering the hold, but whether the leak had sprung afresh, or whether the caulking in some of the seams was insufficient, it was then impossible to determine; all that could be done was to let the ship go with the wind and wait for day.

At daybreak they sounded again:—"Three feet of water!" was the report, I glanced at Curtis, his lips were white, but he had not lost his self-possession. He quietly informed such of the passengers as were already on deck of the new danger that threatened us; it was better that they should know the worst, and the fact could not be long concealed. I told M.

Letourneur that I could not help hoping that there might yet be time to reach the land before the last crisis came. Falsten was about to give vent to an expression of despair, but he was soon silenced by Miss Herbey asserting her confidence that all would yet be well.

Curtis at once divided the crew into two sets, and made them work incessantly, turn and turn about at the pumps. The men applied themselves to their task with resignation rather than with ardour; the labour was hard and scarcely repaid them; the pumps were constantly getting out of order, the valves being choked up by the ashes and bits of cotton that were floating about in the hold, while every moment that was spent in cleaning or repairing them was so much time lost.

Slowly, but surely, the water continued to rise, and on the following morning the soundings gave five feet for its depth, I noticed that Curtis's brow contracted each time that the boatswain or the lieutenant brought him their report. There was no doubt it was only a question of time, and not for an instant must the efforts for keeping down the level be relaxed. Already the ship had sunk a foot lower in the water, and as her weight increased she no longer rose buoyantly with the waves, but pitched and rolled considerably.

All yesterday, and last night, the pumping continued; but still the sea gained upon us. The crew are weary and discouraged, but the second officer and the boatswain set them a fine example of endurance, and the passengers have now begun to take their turn at the pumps.

But all are conscious of toiling almost against hope; we are no longer secured firmly to the solid soil of the Ham Rock reef, but we are floating over an abyss which daily, nay hourly, threatens to swallow us into its depths.

CHAPTER XXIII.

DECEMBER 2nd and 3rd.—For four hours we have succeeded in keeping the water in the hold to one level; now, however, it is very evident that the time cannot be far distant when the pumps will be quite unequal to their task.

Yesterday Curtis, who does not allow himself a minute's rest, made a personal inspection of the hold. I, with the boatswain and carpenter, accompanied him. After dislodging some of the bales of cotton we could hear a splashing, or rather gurgling sound; but whether the water was entering at the original aperture, or whether it found its way in through a general dislocation of the seams, we were unable to discover. But whichever might be the case, Curtis determined to try a plan which, by cutting off communication between the interior and exterior of the vessel, might, if only for a few hours, render her hull more watertight. For this purpose he had some strong, well-tarred sails drawn upwards by ropes from below the keel, as high as the previous leaking-place, and then fastened closely and securely to the side of the hull. The scheme was dubious, and the operation difficult, but for a time it was effectual, and at the close of the day the level of the water had actually been reduced by several inches. The diminution was small enough, but the consciousness that more water was escaping through the scupper-holes than was finding its way into the hold gave us fresh courage to persevere with our work.

The night was dark, but the captain carried all the sail he could, eager to take every possible advantage of the wind, which was freshening considerably. If he could have sighted a ship he would have made signals of distress, and would not have hesitated to transfer the passengers, and even have allowed the crew to follow, if they were ready to forsake him; for himself his mind was made up, he should remain on board the "Chancellor" until she foundered beneath his feet. No sail, however, hove in sight; consequently escape by such means was out of our power.

During the night the canvas covering yielded to the pressure of the waves, and this morning, after taking the sounding, the boatswain could not suppress an oath when he announced "Six feet of water in the hold!"

The ship, then, was filling once again, and already had sunk considerably below her previous water-line. With aching arms and bleeding hands we worked harder than ever at the pumps, and Curtis makes those who are not pumping form a line and pass buckets, with all the speed they can, from hand to hand.

But all in vain! At half-past eight more water is reported in the hold, and some of the sailors, overcome by despair, refuse to work one minute longer.

The first to abandon his post was Owen, a man whom I have mentioned before, as exhibiting something of a mutinous spirit, He is about forty years of age, and altogether unprepossessing in appearance; his face is bare, with the exception of a reddish beard, which terminates in a point; his forehead is furrowed with sinister-looking wrinkles, his lips curl inwards, and his ears protrude, whilst his bleared and bloodshot eyes are encircled with thick red rings.

Amongst the five or six other men who had struck work, I noticed Jynxstrop the cook, who evidently shared all Owen's ill feelings.

Twice did Curtis order the men back to the pumps, and twice did Owen, acting as spokesman for the rest, refuse; and when Curtis made a step forward as though to approach him, he said savagely,—

"I advise you not to touch me," and walked away to the forecastle.

Curtis descended to his cabin, and almost immediately returned with a loaded revolver in his hand.

For a moment Owen surveyed the captain with a frown of defiance; but at a sign from Jynxstrop he seemed to recollect himself; and, with the remainder of the men, he returned to his work.

CHAPTER XXIV.

DECEMBER 4th.—The first attempt at mutiny being thus happily suppressed, it is to be hoped that Curtis will succeed as well in future. An insubordinate crew would render us powerless indeed.

Throughout the night the pumps were kept, without respite, steadily at work, but without producing the least sensible benefit. The ship became so water-logged and heavy that she hardly rose at all to the waves, which consequently often washed over the deck and contributed their part towards aggravating our case. Our situation was rapidly becoming as terrible as it had been when the fire was raging in the midst of us; and the prospect of being swallowed by the devouring billows was no less formidable than that of perishing in the flames.

Curtis kept the men up to the mark, and, willing or unwilling, they had no alternative but to work on as best they might; but, in spite of all their efforts, the water perpetually rose, till, at length, the men in the hold who were passing the buckets found themselves immersed up to their waists and were obliged to come on deck.

This morning, after a somewhat protracted consultation with Walter and the boatswain, Curtis resolved to abandon the ship. The only remaining boat was far too small to hold us all, and it would therefore be necessary to construct a raft that should carry those who could not find room in her. Dowlas the carpenter, Mr. Falsten, and ten sailors were told off to put the raft in hand, the rest of the crew being ordered to continue their work assiduously at the pumps, until the time came and everything was ready for embarkation.

Hatchet or saw in hand, the carpenter and his assistants made a beginning without delay by cutting and trimming the spare yards and extra spars to a proper length. These were then lowered into the sea, which was propitiously calm, so as to favour the operation (which otherwise would have been very difficult) of lashing them together into a firm framework, about forty feet long and twenty-five feet wide, upon which the platform was to be supported.

I kept my own place steadily at the pumps, and Andre Letourneur worked at my side; I often noticed his father glance at him sorrowfully, as though he wondered what would become of him if he had to struggle with waves to which even the strongest man could hardly fail to succumb. But come what may, his father will never forsake him, and I myself shall not be wanting in rendering him whatever assistance I can.

Mrs. Kear, who had been for some time in a state of drowsy unconsciousness, was not informed of the immediate danger, but when Miss Herbey, looking somewhat pale with fatigue, paid one of her flying visits to the deck, I warned her to take every precaution for herself and to be ready for any emergency.

"Thank you, doctor, I am always ready," she cheerfully replied, and returned to her duties below. I saw Andre follow the young girl with his eyes, and a look of melancholy interest passed over his countenance.

Towards eight o'clock in the evening the framework for the raft was almost complete, and the men were lowering empty barrels, which had first been securely bunged, and were lashing them to the wood-work to insure its floating.

Two hours later and suddenly there arose the startling cry, "We are sinking! we are sinking!"

Up to the poop rushed Mr. Kear, followed immediately by Falsten and Miss Herbey, who were bearing the inanimate form of Mrs. Kear. Curtis ran to his cabin, instantly returning with a chart; a sextant, and a compass in his hand.

The scene that followed will ever be engraven in my memory; the cries of distress, the general confusion, the frantic rush of the sailors towards the raft that was not yet ready to support them, can never be forgotten. The whole period of my life seemed to be concentrated into that terrible moment when the planks bent below my feet and the ocean yawned beneath me.

Some of the sailors had taken their delusive refuge in the shrouds, and I was preparing to follow them when a hand was laid upon my shoulder. Turning round I beheld M. Letourneur, with tears in his eyes, pointing towards his son. "Yes, my friend," I said, pressing his hand, "we will save him, if possible."

But Curtis had already caught hold of the young man, and was hurrying him to the main-mast shrouds, when the "Chancellor," which had been scudding along rapidly with the wind, stopped suddenly, with a violent shock, and began to settle, The sea rose over my ankles and almost instinctively I clutched at the nearest rope. All at once, when it seemed all over, the ship ceased to sink, and hung motionless in mid-ocean.

CHAPTER XXV.

NIGHT OF DECEMBER 4th.—Curtis caught young Letourneur again in his arms, and running with him across the flooded deck deposited him safely in the starboard shrouds, whither his father and I climbed up beside him.

I now had time to look about me. The night was not very dark, and I could see that Curtis had returned to his post upon the poop; whilst in the extreme aft near the taffrail, which was still above water, I could distinguish the forms of Mr. and Mrs. Kear, Miss Herbey, and Mr. Falsten The lieutenant and the boatswain were on the far end of the forecastle; the remainder of the crew in the shrouds and top-masts.

By the assistance of his father, who carefully guided his feet up the rigging, Andre was hoisted into the main-top. Mrs. Kear could not be induced to join him in his elevated position, in spite of being told that if the wind were to freshen she would inevitably be washed overboard by the waves; nothing could induce her to listen to remonstrance, and she insisted upon remaining on the poop, Miss Herbey, of course, staying by her side.

As soon as the captain saw the "Chancellor" was no longer sinking, he set to work to take down all the sails, yards and all, and the top-gallants, in the hope that by removing everything that could compromise the equilibrium of the ship he might diminish the chance of her capsizing altogether.

"But may she not founder at any moment?" I said to Curtis, when I had joined him for a while upon the poop.

"Everything depends upon the weather," he replied, in his calmest manner; "that, of course, may change at any hour. One thing, however, is certain, the 'Chancellor' preserves her equilibrium for the present."

"But do you mean to say," I further asked, "that she can sail with two feet of water over her deck?"

"No, Mr. Kazallon, she can't sail, but she can drift with the wind, and if the wind remains in its present quarter, in the course of a few days we might possibly sight the coast. Besides, we shall have our raft as a last resource; in a few hours it will be ready, and at daybreak we can embark."

"You have not then," I added, "abandoned all hope even yet?" I marvelled at his composure.

"While there's life there's hope, you know Mr. Kazallon; out of a hundred chances, ninety-nine may be against us, but perhaps the odd one may be in our favour. Besides, I believe that our case is not without precedent. In the year 1795 a three-master, the 'Juno,' was precisely in the same half-sunk, water-logged condition as ourselves; and yet with her passengers and crew clinging to her top-masts she drifted for twenty days, until she came in sight of land, when those who had survived the deprivation and fatigue were saved. So let us not despair; let us hold on to the hope that the survivors of the 'Chancellor' may be equally fortunate."

I was only too conscious that there was not much to be said in support of Curtis's sanguine view of things, and that the force of reason pointed all the other way; but I said nothing, deriving what comfort I could from the fact that the captain did not yet despond of an ultimate rescue.

As it was necessary to be prepared to abandon the ship almost at a moment's notice, Dowlas was making every exertion to hurry on the construction of the raft. A little before midnight he was on the point of conveying some planks for this purpose, when, to his astonishment and horror, he found that the framework had totally disappeared. The ropes that had attached it to the vessel had snapped as she became vertically displaced, and probably it had been adrift for more than an hour.

The crew were frantic at this new misfortune, and shouting "Overboard with the masts!" they began to cut down the rigging preparatory to taking possession of the masts for a new raft.

But here Curtis interposed:—

"Back to your places, my men; back to your places. The ship will not sink yet, so don't touch a rope until I give you leave."

The firmness of the captain's voice brought the men to their senses, and although some of them could ill disguise their reluctance, all returned to their posts.

When daylight had sufficiently advanced Curtis mounted the mast, and looked around for the missing raft; but it was nowhere to be seen. The sea was far too rough for the men to venture to take out the whaleboat in search of it, and there was no choice but to set to work and to construct a new raft immediately.

Since the sea has become so much rougher, Mrs. Kear has been induced to leave the poop, and has managed to join M. Letourneur and his son on the main-top, where she lies in a state of complete prostration. I need hardly add that Miss Herbey continues in her unwearied attendance. The space to which these four people are limited is necessarily very small, nowhere measuring twelve feet across; to prevent them losing their balance some spars have been lashed from shroud to shroud, and for the convenience of the two ladies Curtis has contrived to make a temporary awning of a sail. Mr. Kear has installed himself with Silas Huntly on the foretop.

A few cases of preserved meat and biscuit and some barrels of water, that floated between the masts after the submersion of the deck, have been hoisted to the top-masts and fastened firmly to the stays. These are now our only provisions.

CHAPTER XXVI.

DECEMBER 5th.—The day was very hot. December in latitude 16deg. N. is a summer month, and unless a breeze should rise to temper the burning sun, we might expect to suffer from an oppressive heat.

The sea still remained very rough, and as the heavy waves broke over the ship as though she were a reef, the foam flew up to the very top-masts, and our clothes were perpetually drenched by the spray.

The "Chancellor's" hull is three-fourths immerged; besides the three masts and the bowsprit, to which the whale-boat was suspended, the poop and the forecastle are the only portions that now are visible; and as the intervening section of the deck is quite below the water, these appear to be connected only by the framework of the netting that runs along the vessel's sides. Communication between the top-masts is extremely difficult, and would be absolutely precluded, were it not that the sailors, with practised dexterity, manage to hoist themselves about by means of the stays. For the passengers, cowering on their narrow and unstable platform, the spectacle of the raging sea below was truly terrific; every wave that dashed over the ship shook the masts till they trembled again, and one could venture scarcely to look or to think lest he should be tempted to cast himself into the vast abyss.

Meanwhile, the crew worked away with all their remaining vigour at the second raft, for which the top-gallants and yards were all obliged to be employed; the planks, too, which were continually being loosened and broken away by the violence of the waves from the partitions of the ship, were rescued before they had drifted out of reach, and were brought into use. The symptoms of the ship foundering did not appear to be immediate; so that Curtis insisted upon the raft being made with proper care to insure its strength; we were still several hundred miles from the coast of Guiana, and for so long a voyage it was indispensable to have a structure of considerable solidity. The reasonableness of this was self-apparent, and as the crew had recovered their assurance they spared no pains to accomplish their work effectually.

Of all the number, there was but one, an Irishman, named O'Ready, who seemed to question the utility of all their toil. He shook his head with an oracular gravity. He is an oldish man, not less than sixty, with his hair and beard bleached with the storms of many travels. As I was making my way towards the poop, he came up to me and began talking.

"And why, bedad, I'd like to know, why is it that they'll all be afther lavin' of the ship?"

He turned his quid with the most serene composure, and continued,—

"And isn't it me myself that's been wrecked nine times already? and sure, poor fools are they that ever have put their trust in rafts or boats sure and they found a wathery grave. Nay, nay; while the ould ship lasts, let's stick to her, says I."

Having thus unburdened his mind he relapsed, into silence, and soon went away.

About three o'clock I noticed that Mr. Kear and Silas Huntly were holding an animated conversation in the fore top. The petroleum merchant had evidently some difficulty in bringing the ex-captain round to his opinion, for I, saw him several times shake his head as he gave long and scrutinizing looks at the sea and sky. In less than an hour afterwards I saw Huntly let himself down by the forestays and clamber along to the forecastle where he joined the group of sailors, and I lost sight of him.

I attached little importance to the incident, and shortly afterwards joined the party in the main-top, where we continued talking for some hours. The heat was intense, and if it had not been for the shelter' afforded by the sail-tent, would have been unbearable. At five o'clock we took as refreshment some dried meat and biscuit, each individual being also allowed half a glass of water. Mrs. Kear, prostrate with fever, could not touch a mouthful; and nothing could be done by Miss Herbey to relieve her, beyond occasionally moistening her parched lips. The unfortunate lady suffers greatly, and sometimes I am inclined to think that she will succumb to the exposure and privation. Not once had her husband troubled himself about her; but when shortly afterwards I heard him hail some of the sailors on the forecastle and ask them to help him down from the foretop, I began to think that the selfish fellow was coming to join his wife.

At first the sailors took no notice of his request, but on his repeating it with the promise of paying them handsomely for their services, two of them, Burke and Sandon, swung themselves along the netting into the shrouds, and were soon at his side.

A long discussion ensued. The men evidently were asking more than Mr. Kear was inclined to give, and at one time if seemed as though the negotiation would fall through altogether. But at length the bargain was struck, and I saw Mr. Kear take a bundle of paper dollars from his waistcoat pocket, and hand a number of them over to one of the men, The man counted them carefully, and from the time it took him, I should think that he could not have pocketed anything less than a hundred dollars.

The next business was to get Mr. Kear down from the foretop, and Burke and Sandon proceeded to tie a rope round his waist, which they afterwards fastened to the forestay; then, in a way which provoked shouts of laughter from their mates, they gave the unfortunate man a shove, and sent him rolling down like a bundle of dirty clothes on to the forecastle.

I was quite mistaken as to his object. Mr. Kear had no intention of looking after his wife, but remained by the side of Silas Huntly until the gathering darkness hid them both from view.

As night drew on, the wind grew calmer, but the sea remained very rough. The moon had been up ever since four in the afternoon, though she only appeared at rare intervals between the clouds. Some long lines of vapour on the horizon were tinged with a rosy glare that foreboded a strong breeze for the morrow, and all felt anxious to know from which quarter the breeze would come, for any but a north-easter would bear the frail raft on which we were to embark far away from land.

About eight o'clock in the evening Curtis mounted to the main-top but he seemed preoccupied and anxious, and did not speak to any one. He remained for a quarter of an hour, then after silently pressing my hand, he returned to his old post.

I laid myself down in the narrow space at my disposal, and tried to sleep; but my mind was filled with strange forebodings, and sleep was impossible. The very calmness of the atmosphere was oppressive; scarcely a breath of air vibrated through the metal rigging, and yet the sea rose with a heavy swell as though it felt the warnings of a coming tempest.

All at once, at about eleven o'clock, the moon burst brightly forth through a rift in the clouds, and the waves sparkled again as if illumined by a submarine glimmer. I start up and look around me. Is it merely imagination? or do I really see a black speck floating on the dazzling whiteness of the waters, a speck that cannot be a rock; because it rises and falls with the heaving motion of the billows? But the moon once again becomes overclouded; the sea, is darkened, and I return to my uneasy couch close to the larboard shrouds.

CHAPTER XXVII.

DECEMBER 6th.—I must have fallen asleep for a few hours, when at four o'clock in the morning, I was rudely aroused by the roaring of the wind, and could distinguish Curtis's voice as he shouted in the brief intervals between the heavy gusts.

I got up, and holding tightly to the purlin—for the waves made the masts tremble with their violence—I tried to look around and below me. The sea was literally raging beneath, and great masses of livid-looking foam were dashing between the masts, which were oscillating terrifically. It was still dark, and I could only faintly distinguish two figures on the stern, whom, by the sound of their voices, that I caught occasionally above the tumult, I made out to be Curtis and the boatswain.

Just at that moment a sailor, who had mounted to the main-top to do something to the rigging, passed close behind me.

"What's the matter?" I asked,

"The wind has changed," he answered, adding something which I could not hear distinctly, but which sounded like "dead against us."

Dead against us! then, thought I, the wind had shifted to the south-west, and my last night's forebodings had been correct.

When daylight at length appeared, I found the wind although not blowing actually from the south-west, had veered round to the north-west, a change which was equally disastrous to us, inasmuch as it was carrying us away from land. Moreover, the ship had sunk considerably during the night, and there were now five feet of water above deck; the side netting had completely disappeared, and the forecastle and the poop were now all but on a level with the sea, which washed over them incessantly. With all possible expedition Curtis and his crew were labouring away at their raft, but the violence of the swell materially impeded their operations, and it became a matter of doubt as to whether the woodwork would not fall asunder before it could be properly fastened together.

As I watched the men at their work M. Letourneur, with one arm supporting his son, came and stood by my side.

"Don't you think this main-top will soon give way?" he said, as the narrow platform on which we stood creaked and groaned with the swaying of the masts.

Miss Herbey heard his words, and pointing towards Mrs. Kear, who was lying prostrate at her feet, asked what we thought ought to be done.

"We can do nothing but stay where we are," I replied.

"No;" said Andre "this is our best refuge; I hope you are not afraid."

"Not for myself," said the young girl quietly "only for those to whom life is precious."

At a quarter to eight we heard the boatswain calling to the sailors in the bows.

"Ay, ay, sir," said one of the men—O'Ready, I think.

"Where's the whale boat?" shouted the boatswain.

"I don't know, sir. Not with us," was the reply.

"She's gone adrift, then!"

And sure enough the whale-boat was no longer hanging from the bowsprit; and in a moment the discovery was made that Mr. Kear, Silas Huntly, and three sailors,—a Scotchman and two Englishmen,—were missing. Afraid that the "Chancellor" would founder before the completion of the raft, Kear and Huntly had plotted together to effect their escape, and had bribed the three sailors to seize the only remaining boat.

This, then, was the black speck that I had seen during the night. The miserable husband had deserted his wife, the faithless captain had abandoned the ship that had once been under his command.

"There are five saved, then," said the boatswain.

"Faith, an it's five lost ye'll be maning," said O'Ready; and the state of the sea fully justified his opinion.

The crew were furious when they heard of the surreptitious flight, and loaded the fugitives with all the invectives they could lay their tongues to. So enraged were they at the dastardly trick of which they had been made the dupes, that if chance should bring the deserters again on board I should be sorry to answer for the consequences.

In accordance with my advice, Mrs. Kear has not been informed of her husband's disappearance. The unhappy lady is wasting away with a fever for which we are powerless to supply a remedy, for the medicine chest was lost when the ship began to sink. Nevertheless, I do not think we have anything to regret on that score, feeling as I do, that in a case like Mrs. Kear's, drugs would be of no avail.

CHAPTER XXVIII.

DECEMBER 6th CONTINUED.—The "Chancellor" no longer maintained her equilibrium; we felt that she was gradually going down, and her hull was probably breaking up. The main-top was already only ten feet above the water, whilst the bowsprit, with the exception of the extreme end, that rose obliquely from the waves, was entirely covered.

The "Chancellor's" last day, we felt, had come.

Fortunately the raft was all but finished, and unless Curtis preferred to wait till morning we should be able to embark in the evening.

The raft is a very solid structure. The spars that form the framework are crossed one above another and lashed together with stout ropes, so that the whole pile rises a couple of feet above the water. The upper platform is constructed from the planks that were broken from the ship's sides by the violence of the waves, and which had not drifted away. The afternoon has been employed in charging the raft with such provisions, sails, tools, and instruments as we have been able to save.

And how can I attempt to give any idea of the feelings with which, one and all, we now contemplated the fate before us? For my own part I was possessed rather by a benumbed indifference than by any sense of genuine resignation. M. Letourneur was entirely absorbed in his son, who, in his turn, thought only of his father; at the same time exhibiting a calm Christian fortitude, which was shown by no one else of the party except Miss Herbey, who faced her danger with the same brave composure. Incredible as it may seem, Falsten remained the same as ever, occupying himself with writing down figures and memoranda in his pocket-book. Mrs. Kear, in spite of all that Miss Herbey could do for her, was evidently dying.

With regard to the sailors, two or three of them were calm enough, but the rest had well-nigh lost their wits. Some of the more ill-disposed amongst them seemed inclined to run into excesses; and their conduct, under the bad influence of Owen and Jynxstrop, made it doubtful whether they would submit to control when once we were limited to the narrow dimensions of the raft. Lieutenant Walter, although his courage never failed him, was worn out with bodily fatigue, and obliged to give up all active labour; but Curtis and the boatswain were resolute, energetic and firm as ever. To borrow an expression from the language of metallurgic art, they were men "at the highest degree of hardness."

At five o'clock one of our companions in misfortune was released from her sufferings. Mrs. Kear, after a most distressing illness, through which her young companion tended her with the most devoted care, has breathed her last. A few deep sighs and all was over, and I doubt whether the sufferer was ever conscious of the peril of, her situation.

The night passed on without further incident. Towards morning I touched the dead woman's hand, and it was cold and stiff. The corpse could not remain any longer on the main-top, and after Miss Herbey and I had carefully wrapped the garments about it, with a few short prayers the body of the first victim of our miseries was committed to the deep.

As the sea closed over the body I heard one of the men in the shrouds say,—

"There goes a carcass that we shall be sorry we have thrown away!"

I looked round sharply. It was Owen who had spoken, But horrible as were his words, the conviction was forced upon my mind that the day could not be far distant when we must want for food.

CHAPTER XXIX.

DECEMBER 7th.—The ship was sinking rapidly; the water had risen to the fore-top; the poop and forecastle were completely submerged; the top of the bowsprit had disappeared, and only the three mast-tops projected from the waves.

But all was ready on the raft; an erection had been made on the fore to hold a mast, which was supported by shrouds fastened to the sides of the platform; this mast carried a large royal.

Perhaps, after all, these few frail planks will carry us to the shore which the "Chancellor" has failed to reach; at any rate, we cannot yet resign all hope.

We were just on the point of embarking at 7 a.m. when the "Chancellor" all at once began to sink so rapidly that the carpenter and men who were on the raft were obliged with all speed to cut the ropes that secured it to the vessel to prevent it from being swallowed up in the eddying waters. Anxiety, the most intense, took possession of us all. At the very moment when the ship was descending into the fathomless abyss, the raft, our only hope of safety, was drifting off before our eyes. Two of the sailors and an apprentice, beside themselves with terror, threw themselves headlong into the sea; but it was evident from the very first that they were quite powerless to combat the winds and waves. Escape was impossible; they could neither reach the raft, nor return to the ship. Curtis tied a rope round his waist and tried to swim to their assistance; but long before he could reach them the unfortunate men, after a vain struggle for life, sank below the waves and were seen no more. Curtis, bruised and beaten with the surf that raged about the mast-heads, was hauled back to the ship.

Meantime, Dowlas and his men, by means of some spars which they used as oars, were exerting themselves to bring back the raft, which had drifted about two cables-lengths away; but, in spite of all their efforts, it was fully an hour,—an hour which seemed to us, waiting as we were with the water up to the level of the top-masts, like an eternity—before they succeeded in bringing the raft alongside, and lashing it once again to the "Chancellor's" main-mast.

Not a moment was then to be lost. The waves were eddying like a whirlpool around the submerged vessel, and numbers of enormous air-bubbles were rising to the surface of the water.

The time was come. At Curtis's word "Embark!" we all hurried to the raft. Andre who insisted upon seeing Miss Herbey go first, was helped safely on to the platform, where his father immediately joined him. In a very few minutes all except Curtis and old O'Ready had left the "Chancellor."

Curtis remained standing on the main-top, deeming it not only his duty, but his right, to be the last to leave the vessel he had loved so well, and the loss of which he so much deplored.

"Now then, old fellow off of this!" cried the captain to the old Irishman, who did not move.

"And is it quite sure ye are that she's sinkin?" he said.

"Ay, ay! sure enough, my man; and you'd better look sharp."

"Faith, then, and I think I will;" and not a moment too soon (for the water was up to his waist) he jumped on to the raft.

Having cast one last, lingering look around him, Curtis then left the ship; the rope was cut and we went slowly adrift.

All eyes were fixed upon the spot where the "Chancellor" lay foundering. The top of the mizzen was the first to disappear, then followed the main-top; and soon, of what had been a noble vessel, not a vestige was to be seen.

CHAPTER XXX.

Will this frail float, forty feet by twenty, bear us in safety? Sink it cannot; the material of which it is composed is of a kind that must surmount the waves. But it is questionable whether it will hold together. The cords that bind it will have a tremendous strain to bear in resisting the violence of the sea. The most sanguine amongst us trembles to face the future; the most confident dares to think only of the present. After the manifold perils of the last seventy-two days' voyage all are too agitated to look forward without dismay to what in all human probability must be a time of the direst distress.

Vain as the task may seem, I will not pause in my work of registering the events of our drama, as scene after scene they are unfolded before our eyes.

Of the twenty-eight persons who left Charleston in the "Chancellor," only eighteen are left to huddle together upon this narrow raft; this number includes the five passengers, namely M. Letourneur, Andre, Miss Herbey, Falsten, and myself; the ship's officers, Captain Curtis, Lieutenant Walter, the boatswain, Hobart the steward, Jynxstrop the cook, and Dowlas the carpenter; and seven sailors, Austin, Owen, Wilson, O'Ready, Burke, Sandon, and Flaypole.

Such are the passengers on the raft; it is but a brief task to enumerate their resources.

The greater part of the provisions in the store-room were destroyed at the time when the ship's deck was submerged, and the small quantity that Curtis has been able to save will be very inadequate to supply the wants of eighteen people, who too probably have many days to wait ere they sight either land or a passing vessel. One cask of biscuit, another of preserved meat, a small keg of brandy, and two barrels of water complete our store, so that the utmost frugality in the distribution of our daily rations becomes absolutely necessary.

Of spare clothes we have positively none; a few sails will serve for shelter by day, and covering by night. Dowlas has his carpenter's tools, we have each a pocket-knife, and O'Ready an old tin pot; of which he takes the most tender care; in addition to these, we are in possession of a sextant, a compass, a chart, and a metal tea-kettle, everything else that was placed on deck in readiness for the first raft having been lost in the partial submersion of the vessel.

Such then is our situation; critical indeed, but after all perhaps not desperate. We have one great fear; some there are amongst us whose courage, moral as well as physical, may give way, and over failing spirits such as these we may have no control.

CHAPTER XXXI.

DECEMBER 7th CONTINUED.—Our first day on the raft has passed without any special incident. At eight o'clock this morning Curtis asked our attention for a moment.

"My friends," he said, "listen to me. Here on this raft, just as when we were on board the 'Chancellor,' I consider myself your captain; and as your captain, I expect that all of you will strictly obey my orders. Let me beg of you, one and all, to think solely of our common welfare; let us work with one heart and with one soul, and may Heaven protect us!"

After delivering these few words with an emotion that evidenced their earnestness, the captain consulted his compass, and found that the freshening breeze was blowing from the north. This was fortunate for us, and no time was to be lost in taking advantage of it to speed us on our dubious way. Dowlas was occupied in fixing the mast into the socket that had already been prepared for its reception, and in order to support it more firmly he placed spurs of wood, forming arched buttresses, on either side. While he was thus employed the boatswain and the other seamen were stretching the large royal sail on the yard that had been reserved for that purpose.

By half-past nine the mast was hoisted, and held firmly in its place by some shrouds attached securely to the sides of the raft; then the sail was run up and trimmed to the wind, and the raft began to make a perceptible progress under the brisk breeze.

As soon as we had once started, the carpenter set to work to contrive some sort of a rudder, that would enable us to maintain our desired direction. Curtis and Falsten assisted him with some serviceable suggestions, and in a couple of hours' time he had made and fixed to the back of the raft a kind of paddle, very similar to those used by the Malays.

At noon, after the necessary preliminary observations, Curtis took the altitude of the sun. The result gave lat. 15deg. 7min. N. by long. 49deg. 35min. W. as our position, which, on consulting the chart, proved to be about 650 miles north-east of the coast of Paramaribo in Dutch Guiana.

Now even under the most favourable circumstances, with trade-winds and weather always in our favour, we cannot by any chance hope to make more than ten or twelve miles a day, so that the voyage cannot possibly be performed under a period of two months. To be sure there is the hope to be indulged that we may fall in with a passing vessel, but as the part of the

Atlantic into which we have been driven is intermediate between the tracks of the French and English Transatlantic steamers either from the Antilles or the Brazils, we cannot reckon at all upon such a contingency happening in our favour; whilst if a calm should set in, or worse still, if the wind were to blow from the east, not only two months, but twice, nay, three times that length of time will be required to accomplish the passage.

At best, however, our provisions, even though used with the greatest care, will barely last three months. Curtis has called us into consultation, and as the working of the raft does not require such labour as to exhaust our physical strength, all have agreed to submit to a regimen which, although it will suffice to keep us alive, will certainly not fully satisfy the cravings of hunger and thirst.

As far as we can estimate, we have somewhere about 500 lbs. of meat and about the same quantity of biscuit. To make this last for three months we ought not to consume very much more than 5 lbs. a day of each, which, when divided among eighteen people, will make the daily ration 5 oz. of meat and 5 oz. of biscuit for each person. Of water we have certainly not more than 200 gallons, but by reducing each person's allowance to a pint a day, we hope to eke out that, too, over the space of three months.

It is arranged that the food shall be distributed under the boatswain's superintendence every morning at ten o'clock. Each person will then receive his allowance of meat and biscuit, which may be eaten when and how he pleases. The water will be given out twice a day—at ten in the morning and six in the evening; but as the only drinking-vessels in our possession are the tea-kettle and the old Irishman's tin pot, the water has to be consumed immediately on distribution. As for the brandy, of which there are only five gallons, it will be doled out with the strictest limitation, and no one will be allowed to touch it except with the captain's express permission.

I should not forget that there are two sources from which we may hope to increase our store. First, any rain that may fall will add to our supply of water, and two empty barrels have been placed ready to receive it; secondly, we hope to do something in the way of fishing, and the sailors have already begun to prepare some lines.

All have mutually agreed to abide by the rules that have been laid down, for all are fully aware that by nothing but the most precise regimen can we hope to avert the horrors of famine, and forewarned by the fate, of many who in similar circumstances have miserably perished, we are determined to do all that prudence can suggest for husbanding our stores.

CHAPTER XXXII.

DECEMBER 8th to 17th.—When night came we wrapped ourselves in our sails. For my own part, worn out with the fatigue of the long watch in the top-mast, I slept for several hours; M. Letourneur and Andre did the same, and Miss Herbey obtained sufficient rest to relieve the tired expression that her countenance had lately been wearing. The night passed quietly. As the raft was not very heavily laden the waves did not break over it at all, and we were consequently able to keep ourselves perfectly dry. To say the truth, it was far better for us that the sea should remain somewhat boisterous, for any diminution in the swell of the waves would indicate that; the wind had dropped, and it was with a feeling of regret that when the morning came I had to note down "weather calm" in my journal.

In these low latitudes the heat in the day-time is so intense, and the sun burns with such an incessant glare, that the entire atmosphere becomes pervaded with a glowing vapour. The wind, too, blows only in fitful gusts and through long intervals of perfect calm the sails flap idly and uselessly against the mast. Curtis and the boatswain, however, are of opinion that we are not entirely dependent on the wind. Certain indications, which a sailor's eye alone could detect, make them almost sure that we are being carried along by a westerly current, that flows at the rate of three or four miles an hour. If they are not mistaken, this is a circumstance that may materially assist our progress, and at which we can hardly fail to rejoice, for the high temperature often makes our scanty allowance of water quite inadequate to allay our thirst.

But with all our hardships I must confess that our condition is far preferable to what it was when we were still clinging to the "Chancellor." Here at least we have a comparatively solid platform beneath our feet, and we are relieved from the incessant dread of being carried down with a foundering vessel. In the day-time we can move about with a certain amount of freedom, discuss the weather, watch the sea, and examine our fishing-lines; whilst at night we can rest securely under the shelter of our sails.

"I really think, Mr. Kazallon," said Andre Letourneur to me a few days after we had embarked, "that our time on board the raft passes as pleasantly as it did upon Ham Rock; and the raft has one advantage even over the reef, for it is capable of motion."

"Yes, Andre," replied, "as long as the wind continues favourable the raft has decidedly the advantage; but supposing the wind shifts, what then?"

"Oh, we mustn't think about that," he said; "let us keep up our courage while we can."

I felt that he was right, and that the dangers we had escaped should make us more hopeful for the future; and I think that nearly all of us are inclined to share his opinion.

Whether the captain is equally sanguine I am unable to say. He holds himself very much aloof, and as he evidently feels that he has the great responsibility of saving other lives than his own, we are reluctant to disturb his silent meditations.

Such of the crew as are not on watch spend the greater portion of their time in dozing on the fore part of the raft. The aft, by the captain's orders, has been reserved for the use of us passengers, and by erecting some uprights we have contrived to make a sort of tent, which affords some shelter from the burning sun. On the whole our bill of health is tolerably satisfactory. Lieutenant Walter is the only invalid, and he, in spite of all our careful nursing, seems to get weaker every day.

Andre Letourneur is the life of our party, and I have never appreciated the young man so well. His originality of perception makes his conversation both lively and entertaining and as he talks, his wan and suffering countenance lights up with an intelligent animation. His father seems to become more devoted to him than ever, and I have seen him sit for an hour at a time, with his hand resting on his son's, listening eagerly to his every word.

Miss Herbey occasionally joins in our conversation, but although we all do our best to make her forget that she has lost those who should have been her natural protectors, M. Letourneur is the only one amongst us to whom she speaks without a certain reserve. To him, whose age gives him something of the authority of a father, she has told the history of her life— a life of patience and self-denial such as not unfrequently falls to the lot of orphans. She had been, she said, two years with Mrs. Kear, and although now left alone in the world, homeless and without resources, hope for the future does not fail her. The young lady's modest deportment and energy of character command the respect of all on board, and I do not think that even the coarsest of the sailors has either by word or gesture acted towards her in a way that she could deem offensive.

The 12th, 13th, and 14th of December passed away without any change in our condition. The wind continued to blow in irregular gusts, but always in the same direction, and the helm, or rather the paddle at the back of the raft has never once required shifting; and the watch, who are posted on the fore, under orders to examine the sea with the most scrupulous attention, have had no change of any kind to report.

At the end of a week we found ourselves growing accustomed to our limited diet, and as we had no manual exertion, and no wear and tear of our physical constitution, we managed very well. Our greatest deprivation was the short supply of water, for, as I said before, the unmitigated heat made our thirst at times very painful.

On the 15th we held high festival. A shoal of fish, of the sparus tribe, swarmed round the raft, and although our tackle consisted merely of long cords baited with morsels of dried meat stuck upon bent nails, the fish were so voracious that in the course of a couple of days we had caught as many as weighed almost 200lbs., some of which were grilled, and others boiled in sea-water over a fire made on the fore part of the raft. This marvelous haul was doubly welcome, inasmuch as it not only afforded us a change of diet, but enabled us to economize our stores; if only some rain had fallen at the same time we should have been more than satisfied.

Unfortunately the shoal of fish did not remain long in our vicinity. On the 17th they all disappeared, and some sharks, not less than twelve or fifteen feet long, belonging to the species of spotted dog-fish, took their place. These horrible creatures have black backs and fins, covered with white spots and stripes. Here, on our low raft, we seem almost on a level with them, and more than once their tails have struck the spars with terrible violence. The sailors manage to keep them at a distance by means of handspikes, but I shall not be surprised if they persist in following us, instinctively intelligent that we are destined to become their prey. For myself, I confess that they give me a feeling of uneasiness; they seem to me like monsters of ill-omen.

CHAPTER XXXIII.

DECEMBER 18th to 20th.—On the 18th the wind freshened a little, but as it blew from the same favourable quarter we did not complain, and only took the precaution of putting an extra support to the mast, so that it should not snap with the tension of the sail. This done, the raft was carried along with something more than its ordinary speed, and left a long line of foam in its wake.

In the afternoon the sky became slightly overclouded, and the heat consequently somewhat less oppressive. The swell made it more difficult for the raft to keep its balance, and we shipped two or three heavy seas; but the carpenter managed to make with some planks a kind of wall about a couple of feet high, which protected us from the direct action of the waves. Our casks of food and water were secured to the raft with double ropes, for we dared not run the risk of their being carried overboard, an accident that would at once have reduced us to the direst distress.

In the course of the day the sailors gathered some of the marine plants known by the name of sargassos, very similar to those we saw in such profusion between the Bermudas and Ham Rock. I advised my companions to chew the laminary tangles, which they would find contained a saccharine juice, affording considerable relief to their parched lips and throats.

The remainder of the day passed without incident. I should not, however, omit to mention that the frequent conferences held amongst the sailors, especially between Owen, Burke, Flaypole, Wilson, and Jynxstrop, the negro, aroused some uneasy suspicions in my mind. What was the subject of their conversation I could not discover, for they became silent immediately that a passenger or one of the officers approached them. When I mentioned the matter to Curtis I found he had already noticed these secret interviews, and that they had given him enough concern to make him determined to keep a strict eye upon Jynxstrop and Owen, who, rascals as they were themselves, were evidently trying to disaffect their mates.

On the 19th the heat was again excessive. The sky was cloudless, and as there was not enough wind to fill the sail the raft lay motionless upon the surface of the water. Some of the sailors found a transient alleviation for their thirst by plunging into the sea, but as we were fully aware that the water all round was infested with sharks, none of us was rash enough to follow their example, though if, as seems likely, we remain long becalmed, we shall probably in time overcome our fears, and feel constrained to indulge ourselves with a bath.

The health of Lieutenant Walter continues to cause us grave anxiety, the young man being weakened by attacks of intermittent fever. Except for the loss of the medicine-chest we might have temporarily reduced this by quinine; but it is only too evident that the poor fellow is consumptive, and that that hopeless malady is making ravages upon him that no medicine could permanently arrest. His sharp dry cough, his short breathing, his profuse perspirations, more especially in the morning; the pinched-in nose, the hollow cheeks, of which the general pallour is only relieved by a hectic flush, the contracted lips, the too brilliant eye and wasted form—all bear witness to a slow but sure decay.

To-day, the 20th, the temperature is as high as ever, and the raft still motionless. The rays of the sun penetrate even through the shelter of our tent, where we sit literally gasping with the heat. The impatience with which we awaited the moment when the boatswain should dole out our meagre allowance of water, and the eagerness with which those lukewarm drops were swallowed, can only be realized by those who for themselves have endured the agonies of thirst.

Lieutenant Walter suffers more than any of us from the scarcity of water, and I noticed that Miss Herbey reserved almost the whole of her own share for his use. Kind and compassionate as ever, the young girl does all that lies in her power to relieve the poor fellow's sufferings.

"Mr. Kazallon," she said to me this morning, "that young man gets manifestly weaker every day."

"Yes, Miss Herbey," I replied, "and how sorrowful it is that we can do nothing for him, absolutely nothing."

"Hush!" she said, with her wonted consideration, "perhaps he will hear what we are saying."

And then she sat down near the edge of the raft, where, with her head resting on her hands, she remained lost in thought.

An incident sufficiently unpleasant occurred to-day. For nearly an hour Owen, Flaypole, Burke, and Jynxstrop had been engaged in close conversation and, although their voices were low, their gestures had betrayed that they were animated by some strong excitement. At the conclusion of the colloquy Owen got up and walked deliberately to the quarter of the raft that has been reserved for the use of the passengers.

"Where are you off to now, Owen?" said the boatswain.

"That's my business," said the man insolently, and pursued his course.

The boatswain was about to stop him, but before he could interfere Curtis was standing and looking Owen steadily in the face.

"Ah, captain, I've got a word from my mates to say to you," he said, with all the effrontery imaginable.

"Say on, then," said the captain coolly.

"We should like to know about that little keg of brandy. Is it being kept for the porpoises or the officers?"

Finding that he obtained no reply, he went on,—

"Look here, captain, what we want is to have our grog served out every morning as usual."

"Then you certainly will not," said the captain.

"What! what!" exclaimed Owen, "don't you mean to let us have our grog?"

"Once and for all, no."

For a moment, with a malicious grin upon his lips, Owen stood confronting the captain; then, as though thinking better of himself, he turned round and rejoined his companions, who were still talking together in an undertone.

When I was afterwards discussing the matter with Curtis I asked him whether he was sure he had done right in refusing the brandy.

"Right!" he cried, "to be sure I have. Allow those men to have brandy! I would throw it all overboard first."

CHAPTER XXXIV.

DECEMBER 21st.—No further disturbance has taken place amongst the men. For a few hours the fish appeared again, and we caught a great many of them, and stored them away in an empty barrel. This addition to our stock of provisions makes us hope that food, at least, will not fail us.

Usually the nights in the tropics are cool, but to-day, as evening drew on, the wonted freshness did not return, but the air remained stifling and oppressive, whilst heavy masses of vapour hung over the water.

There was no moonlight; there would be a new moon at half-past one in the morning, but the night was singularly dark, except for dazzling flashes of summer lightning that from time to time illumined the horizon far and wide. There was, however, no answering roll of thunder, and the silence of the atmosphere seemed almost awful, For a couple of hours, in the vain hope of catching a breath of air, Miss Herbey, Andre Letourneur, and I, sat watching the imposing struggle of the electric vapours. The clouds appeared like embattled turrets crested with flame, and the very sailors, coarse-minded men as they were, seemed struck with the grandeur of the spectacle, and regarded attentively, though with an anxious eye, the preliminary tokens of a coming storm. Until midnight we kept our seats upon the stern of the raft, whilst the lightning ever and again shed around us a livid glare similar to that produced by adding salt to lighted alcohol.

"Are you afraid of a storm, Miss Herbey?" said Andre to the girl.

"No, Mr. Andre, my feelings are always rather those of awe than of fear," she replied. "I consider a storm one of the sublimest phenomena that we can behold—don't you think so too?"

"Yes, and especially when the thunder is pealing," he said; "that majestic rolling, far different to the sharp crash of artillery, rises and falls like the long-drawn notes of the grandest music, and I can safely say that the tones of the most accomplished ARTISTE have never moved me like that incomparable voice of nature."

"Rather a deep bass, though," I said, laughing.

"That may be," he answered; "but I wish we might hear it now, for this silent lightning is somewhat unexpressive."

"Never mind that, Andre" I said; "enjoy a storm when it comes, if you like, but pray don't wish for it."

"And why not?" said he; "a storm will bring us wind, you know."

"And water, too," added Miss Herbey, "the water of which we are so seriously in need."

The young people evidently wished to regard the storm from their own point of view, and although I could have opposed plenty of common sense to their poetical sentiments, I said no more, but let them talk on as they pleased for fully an hour.

Meantime the sky was becoming quite overclouded, and after the zodiacal constellations had disappeared in the mists that hung round the horizon, one by one the stars above our heads were veiled in dark rolling masses of vapour, from which every instant there issued forth sheets of electricity that formed a vivid background to the dark grey fragments of cloud that floated beneath.

As the reservoir of electricity was confined to the higher strata of the atmosphere, the lightning was still unaccompanied by thunder; but the dryness of the air made it a weak conductor. Evidently the fluid could only escape by terrible shocks, and the storm must ere long burst forth with fearful violence.

This was the opinion of Curtis and the boatswain. The boatswain is only weather-wise from his experience as a sailor; but Curtis, in addition to his experience, has some scientific knowledge, and he pointed out to me an appearance in the sky known to meteorologists as a "cloud-ring," and scarcely ever seen beyond the regions of the torrid zone, which are impregnated by damp vapours brought from all quarters of the ocean by the action of the trade-winds.

"Yes, Mr. Kazallon," said Curtis, "our raft has been driven into the region of storms, of which it has been justly remarked that any one endowed with very sensitive organs can at any moment distinguish the growlings of thunder."

"Hark!" I said, as I strained my ears to listen, "I think I can hear it now."

"You can," he answered; "yet what you hear is but the first warning of the storm which, in a couple of hours, will burst upon us with all its fury. But never mind, we must be ready for it."

Sleep, even if we wished it, would have been impossible in that stifling temperature. The lightning increased in brilliancy, and appeared from all quarters of the horizon, each flash covering large arcs, varying from 100deg. to 150deg., leaving the atmosphere pervaded by one incessant phosphorescent glow.

The thunder became at length more and more distinct, the reports, if I may use the expression, being "round," rather than rolling. It seemed almost as though the sky were padded with heavy clouds of which the elasticity muffled the sound of the electric bursts.

Hitherto, the sea had been calm, almost stagnant as a pond. Now, however, long undulations took place, which the sailors recognized, all too well, as being the rebound produced by a distant tempest. A ship, in such a case, would have been instantly brought ahull, but no manoeuvring could be applied to our raft, which could only drift before the blast.

At one o'clock in the morning one vivid flash, followed, after the interval of a few seconds, by a loud report of thunder, announced that the storm was rapidly approaching. Suddenly the horizon was enveloped in a vapourous fog, and seemed to contract until it was close around us. At the same instant the voice of one of the sailors was heard shouting,—

"A squall! a squall!"

CHAPTER XXXV.

DECEMBER 21st, NIGHT.—The boatswain rushed to the halliards that supported the sail, and instantly lowered the yard; and not a moment too soon, for with the speed of an arrow the squall was upon us, and if it had not been for the sailor's timely warning we must all have been knocked down and probably precipitated into the sea; as it was, our tent on the back of the raft was carried away.

The raft itself, however, being so nearly level with the water, had little peril to encounter from the actual wind; but from the mighty waves now raised by the hurricane we had everything to dread. At first the waves had been crushed and flattened as it were by the pressure of the air, but now, as though strengthened by the reaction, they rose with the utmost fury. The raft followed the motions of the increasing swell, and was tossed up and down, to and fro, and from side to side with the most violent oscillations "Lash yourselves tight," cried the boatswain, as he threw us some ropes; and in a few moments, with Curtis's assistance, M. Letourneur, Andre, Falsten, and myself were fastened so firmly to the raft, that nothing but its total disruption could carry us away. Miss Herbey was bound by a rope passed round her waist to one of the uprights that had supported our tent, and by the glare of the lightning I could see that her countenance was as serene and composed as ever.

Then the storm began to rage indeed. Flash followed flash, peal followed peal in quick succession. Our eyes were blinded, our ears deafened, with the roar and glare. The clouds above, the ocean beneath, seemed verily to have taken fire, and several times I saw forked lightnings dart upwards from the crest of the waves, and mingle with those that radiated from the fiery vault above. A strong odour of sulphur pervaded the air, but though thunderbolts fell thick around us, not one had touched our raft.

By two o'clock the storm had reached its height. The hurricane had increased, and the heavy waves, heated to a strange heat by the general temperature, dashed over us until we were drenched to the skin. Curtis, Dowlas, the boatswain, and the sailors did what they could to strengthen the raft with additional ropes. M. Letourneur placed himself in front of Andre to shelter him from the waves. Miss Herbey stood upright and motionless as a statue.

Soon dense masses of lurid clouds came rolling up, and a crackling, like the rattle of musketry, resounded through the air. This was produced by a series of electrical concussions, in which volleys of hailstones were discharged from the cloud-batteries above. In fact, as the storm-sheet came in contact with a current of cold air, hail was formed with great rapidity, and hailstones, large as nuts, came pelting down, making the platform of the raft re-echo with a metallic ring.

For about half an hour the meteoric shower continued to descend, and during that time the wind slightly abated in violence; but after having shifted from quarter to quarter, it once more blew with all its former fury. The shrouds were broken, but happily the mast, already bending almost double, was removed by the men from its socket before it should be snapped short off. One gust caught away the tiller, which went adrift beyond all power of recovery, and the same blast blew down several of the planks that formed the low parapet on the larboard side, so that the waves dashed in without hindrance through the breach.

The carpenter and his mates tried to repair the damage, but, tossed from wave to wave, the raft was inclined to an angle of more than forty-five degrees, making it impossible for them to keep their footing, and rolling one over another, they were thrown down by the violent shocks. Why they were not altogether carried away, why we were not all hurled into the sea, was to me a mystery. Even if the cords that bound us should retain their hold, it seemed perfectly incredible that the raft itself should not be overturned, so that we should be carried down and stifled in the seething waters.

At last, towards three in the morning, when the hurricane seemed to be raging more fiercely than ever, the raft, caught up on the crest of an enormous wave, stood literally perpendicularly on its edge. For an instant, by the illumination of the lightning, we beheld ourselves raised to an incomprehensible height above the foaming breakers. Cries of terror escaped our lips. All must be over now! But no; another moment, and the raft had resumed its horizontal position. Safe, indeed, we were, but the tremendous upheaval was not without its melancholy consequences. The cords that secured the cases of provisions had burst asunder. One case rolled overboard, and the side of one of the water-barrels was staved in, so that the water which it contained was rapidly escaping. Two of the sailors rushed forward to rescue the case of preserved meat; but one of them caught his foot between the planks of the platform, and, unable to disengage it, the poor fellow stood uttering-cries of distress.

I tried to go to his assistance, and had already untied the cord that was round me; but I was too late. Another heavy sea dashed over us, and by the light of a dazzling flash I saw the unhappy man, although he had managed without assistance to disengage his foot, washed overboard before it was in my power to get near him. His companion had also disappeared.

The same ponderous wave laid me prostrate on the platform, and as my head came in collision with the corner of a spar, for a time I lost all consciousness.

CHAPTER XXXVI.

DECEMBER 22nd.—Daylight came at length, and the sun broke through and dispersed the clouds that the storm had left behind. The struggle of the elements, while it lasted, had been terrific, but the swoon into which I was thrown by my fall, prevented me from observing the final incidents of the visitation. All that I know is, that shortly after we had shipped the heavy sea that I have mentioned, a shower of rain had the effect of calming the severity of the hurricane, and tended to diminish the electric tension of the atmosphere.

Thanks to the kind care of M. Letourneur and Miss Herbey, I recovered consciousness, but I believe that it is to Robert Curtis that I owe my real deliverance, for he it was that prevented me from being carried away by a second heavy wave.

The tempest, fierce as it was, did not last more than a few hours, but even in that short space of time what an irreparable loss we have sustained, and what a load of misery seems stored up for us in the future!

Of the two sailors who perished in the storm, one was Austin, a fine active young man of about eight-and-twenty; the other was old O'Ready, the survivor of so many ship wrecks. Our party is thus reduced to sixteen souls, leaving a total barely exceeding half the number of those who embarked on board the "Chancellor" at Charleston.

Curtis's first care had been to take a strict account of the remnant of our provisions. Of all the torrents of rain that fell in the night we were unhappily unable to catch a single drop; but water will not fail us yet, for about fourteen gallons still remain in the bottom of the broken barrel, whilst the second barrel has not yet been touched. But of food we have next to nothing. The cases containing the dried meat, and the fish that we had preserved, have both been washed away, and all that now remains to us is about sixty pounds of biscuit. Sixty pounds of biscuit between sixteen persons! Eight days, with half a pound a day apiece, will consume it all.

The day has passed away in silence. A general depression has fallen upon all: the spectre of famine has appeared amongst us, and each has remained wrapped in his own gloomy meditations, though each has doubtless but one idea dominant in his mind.

Once, as I passed near the group of sailors lying on the fore part of the raft, I heard Flaypole say with a sneer,—

"Those who are going to die had better make haste about it."

"Yes," said Owen, "leave their share of food to others."

At the regular hour each person received his half-pound of biscuit. Some, I noticed, swallowed it ravenously, others reserved it for another time. Falsten divided his ration into several portions, corresponding, I believe, to the number of meals to which he was ordinarily accustomed. What prudence he shows! If any one survives this misery, I think it will be he.

CHAPTER XXXVII.

DECEMBER 23rd to 30th—After the storm the wind settled back into its old quarter, blowing pretty briskly from the north-east. As the breeze was all in our favour it was important to make the most of it, and after Dowlas had carefully readjusted the mast, the sail was once more hoisted, and we were carried along at the rate of two or two and a half knots an hour. A new rudder, formed of a spar and a good-sized plank, has been fitted in the place of the one we lost, but with the wind in its present quarter it is in little requisition. The platform of the raft has been repaired, the disjointed planks have been closed by means of ropes and wedges, and that portion of the parapet that was washed away has been replaced, so that we are no longer wetted by the waves. In fact, nothing has been left undone to insure the solidity of our raft, and to render it capable of resisting the wear and tear of the wind and waves. But the dangers of wind and waves are not those which we have most to dread.

Together with the unclouded sky came a return of the tropical heat, which during the preceding days had caused us such serious inconvenience; fortunately on the 23rd the excessive warmth was somewhat tempered by the breeze, and as the tent was once again put up, we were able to find shelter under it by turns.

But the want of food was beginning to tell upon us sadly, and our sunken cheeks and wasted forms were visible tokens of what we were enduring. With most of us hunger seemed to attack the entire nervous system, and the constriction of the stomach produced an acute sensation of pain. A narcotic, such as opium or tobacco, might have availed to soothe, if not to cure, the gnawing agony; but of sedatives we had none, so the pain must be endured.

One alone there was amongst us who did not feel the pangs of hunger. Lieutenant Walter seemed as it were to feed upon the fever that raged within him; but then he was the victim of the most torturing thirst, Miss Herbey, besides reserving for him a portion of her own insufficient allowance, obtained from the captain a small extra supply of water, with which every quarter of an hour she moistened the parched lips of the young man, who almost too weak to speak, could only express his thanks by a grateful smile. Poor fellow! all our care cannot avail to save him now; he is doomed, most surely doomed to die.

On the 23rd he seemed to be conscious of his condition, for he made a sign to me to sit down by his side, and then summoning up all his strength to speak, he asked me in a few broken words how long I thought he had to live? Slight as my hesitation was, Walter noticed it immediately.

"The truth," he said; "tell me the plain truth."

"My dear fellow, I am not a doctor, you know," I began, "and I can scarcely judge—"

"Never mind," he interrupted, "tell me just what you think."

I looked at him attentively for some moments, then laid my ear against his chest. In the last few days his malady had made fearfully rapid strides, and it was only too evident that one lung had already ceased to act, whilst the other was scarcely capable of performing the work of respiration. The young man was now suffering from the fever which is the sure symptom of the approaching end in all tuberculous complaints.

The lieutenant kept his eye fixed upon me with a look of eager inquiry. I knew not what to say, and sought to evade his question.

"My dear boy," I said, "in our present circumstances not one of us can tell how long he has to live. Not one of us knows what may happen in the course of the next eight days."

"The next eight days," he murmured, as he looked eagerly into my face.

And then, turning away his head, he seemed to fall into a sort of doze.

The 24th, 25th, and 26th passed without any alteration in our circumstances, and strange, nay, incredible as it may sound, we began to get accustomed to our condition of starvation. Often, when reading the histories of shipwrecks, I have suspected the accounts to be greatly exaggerated; but now I fully realize their truth, and marvel when I find on how little nutriment it is possible to exist for so long a time. To our daily half-pound of biscuit the captain has thought to add a few drops of brandy, and the stimulant helps considerably to sustain our strength. If we had the same provisions for two months, or even for one, there might be room for hope; but our supplies diminish rapidly, and the time is fast approaching when of food and drink there will be none.

The sea had furnished us with food once, and, difficult as the task of fishing had now become, at all hazards the attempt must be made again. Accordingly the carpenter and the boatswain set to work and made lines out of some untwisted hemp, to which they fixed some nails that they pulled out of the flooring of the raft, and bent into proper shape. The boatswain regarded his device with evident satisfaction.

"I don't mean to say," said he to me, "that these nails are first-rate fish-hooks; but one thing I do know, and that is, with proper bait they will act as well as the best. But this biscuit is no good at all. Let me but just get hold of one fish, and I shall know fast enough how to use it to catch some more."

And the true difficulty was how to catch the first fish. It was evident that fish were not abundant in these waters, nevertheless the lines were cast. But the biscuit with which they were baited dissolved at once in the water, and we did not get a single bite. For two days the attempt was made in vain, and as it only involved what seemed a lavish waste of our only means of subsistence, it was given up in despair.

To-day, the 30th, as a last resource, the boatswain tried what a piece of coloured rag might do by way of attracting some voracious fish, and having obtained from Miss Herbey a little piece of the red shawl she wears, he fastened it to his hook. But still no success; for when, after several hours, he examined his lines, the crimson shred was still hanging intact as he had fixed it. The man was quite discouraged at his failure.

"But there will be plenty of bait before long," he said to me in a solemn undertone.

"What do you mean?" said I, struck by his significant manner.

"You'll know soon enough," he answered.

What did he insinuate? The words, coming from a man usually so reserved, have haunted me all night.

CHAPTER XXXVIII.

JANUARY 1st to 5th.—More than three months had elapsed since we left Charleston in the "Chancellor," and for no less than twenty days had we now been borne along on our raft at the mercy of the wind and waves. Whether we were approaching the American coast, or whether we were drifting farther and farther to sea, it was now impossible to determine, for, in addition to the other disasters caused by the hurricane, the captain's instruments had been hopelessly smashed, and Curtis had no longer any compass by which to direct his course, nor a sextant by which he might make an observation.

Desperate, however, as our condition might be judged, hope did not entirely abandon our hearts, and day after day, hour after hour were our eyes strained towards the horizon, and many and many a time did our imagination shape out the distant land. But ever and again the illusion vanished; a cloud, a mist, perhaps even a wave, was all that had deceived us; no land, no sail ever broke the grey line that united sea and sky, and our raft remained the centre of the wide and dreary waste.

On the 1st of January we swallowed our last morsel of biscuit. The 1st of January! New Year's Day! What a rush of sorrowful recollections overwhelmed our minds! Had we not always associated the opening of another year with new hopes, new plans, and coming joys? And now, where were we? Could we dare to look at one another, and breathe a new year's greeting?

The boatswain approached me with a peculiar look on his countenance.

"You are surely not going to wish me a happy new year?" I said.

"No indeed, sir," he replied, "I was only going to wish you well through the first day of it; and that is pretty good assurance on my part, for we have not another crumb to eat."

True as it was, we scarcely realized the fact of there being actually nothing until on the following morning the hour came round for the distribution of the scanty ration, and then, indeed, the truth was forced upon us in a new and startling light. Towards evening I was seized with violent pains in the stomach, accompanied by a constant desire to yawn and gape that was most distressing; but in a couple of hours the extreme agony passed away, and on the 3rd I was surprised to find that I did not suffer more. I felt, it is true, that there was some great void within myself, but the sensation was quite as much moral as physical. My head was so heavy that I could not hold it up; it was swimming with giddiness, as though I were looking over a precipice.

My symptoms were not shared by all my companions, some of whom endured the most frightful tortures. Dowlas and the boatswain especially, who were naturally large eaters, uttered involuntary cries of agony, and were obliged to gird themselves tightly with ropes to subdue the excruciating pain that was gnawing their very vitals.

And this was only the second day of our misery! what would we not have given for half, nay, for a quarter of the meagre ration which a few days back we had deemed so inadequate to supply our wants, and which now, eked out crumb by crumb, might, perhaps, serve for several days? In the streets of a besieged city, dire as the distress may be, some gutter, some rubbish-heap, some corner may yet be found that will furnish a dry bone or a scrap of refuse that may for a moment allay the pangs of hunger; but these bare planks, so many times washed clean by the relentless waves, offer nothing to our eager search, and after every fragment of food that the wind carried into their interstices has been scraped out devoured, our resources are literally at an end.

The nights seem even longer than the days. Sleep, when it comes, brings no relief; it is rather a feverish stupour, broken and disturbed by frightful nightmares. Last night, however, overcome by fatigue, I managed to rest for several hours.

At six o'clock this morning I was roused by the sound of angry voices, and, starting up, I saw Owen and Jynxstrop, with Flaypole, Wilson, Burke, and Sandon, standing in a threatening attitude. They had taken possession of the carpenter's tools, and now, armed with hatchets, chisels, and hammers, they were preparing to attack the captain, the boatswain, and Dowlas. I attached myself in a moment to Curtis's party. Falsten followed my example, and although our knives were the only weapons at our disposal, we were ready to defend ourselves to the very last extremity.

Owen and his men advanced towards us. The miserable wretches were all drunk, for during the night they had knocked a hole in the brandy-barrel, and had recklessly swallowed its contents. What they wanted they scarcely seemed to know, but Owen and Jynxstrop, not quite so much intoxicated as the rest; seemed to be urging them on to massacre the captain and the officers.

"Down with the captain! Overboard with Curtis! Owen shall take the command!" they shouted from time to time in their drunken fury; and, armed as they were, they appeared completely masters of the situation.

"Now, then, down with your arms!" said Curtis sternly, as he advanced to meet them.

"Overboard with the captain!" howled Owen, as by word and gesture he urged on his accomplices.

Curtis' pushed aside the excited rascals, and, walking straight up to Owen, asked him what he wanted.

"What do we want? Why, we want no more captains; we are all equals now."

Poor stupid fool! as though misery and privation had not already reduced us all to the same level.

"Owen," said the captain once, again, "down with your arms!"

"Come on, all of you," shouted Owen to his companions, without giving the slightest heed to Curtis's words.

A regular struggle ensued. Owen and Wilson attacked Curtis, who defended himself with a piece of a spar; Burke and Flaypole rushed upon Falsten and the boatswain, whilst I was left to confront the negro Jynxstrop, who attempted to strike me with the hammer which he brandished in his hand. I endeavoured to paralyze his movements by pinioning his arms, but the rascal was my superior in muscular strength. After wrestling for a few moments, I felt that he was getting the mastery over me when all of a sudden he rolled over on to the platform, dragging me with him. Andre Letourneur had caught hold of one of his legs, and thus saved my life. Jynxstrop dropped his weapon in his fall; I seized it instantly, and was about to cleave the fellow's skull, when I was myself arrested by Andre's hand upon my arm.

By this time the mutineers had been driven back to the forepart of the raft, and Curtis, who had managed to parry the blows which had been aimed at him, had caught hold of a hatchet, with which he was preparing to strike at Owen. But Owen made a sidelong movement to avoid the blow, and the weapon caught Wilson full in the chest. The unfortunate man rolled over the side of the raft and instantly disappeared.

"Save him! save him!" shouted the boatswain.

"It's too late; he's dead!" said Dowlas.

"Ah, well! he'll do for—" began the boatswain; but he did not finish his sentence.

Wilson's death, however, put an end to the fray. Flaypole and Burke were lying prostrate in a drunken stupour, and Jynxstrop was soon overpowered, and lashed tightly to the foot of the mast. The carpenter and the boatswain seized hold of Owen.

"Now then," said Curtis, as he raised his blood-stained hatchet, "make your peace with God, for you have not a moment to live."

"Oh, you want to eat me, do you?" sneered Owen, with the most hardened effrontery.

But the audacious reply saved his life; Curtis turned as pale as death, the hatchet dropped from his hand, and he went and seated himself moodily on the farthest corner of the raft.

CHAPTER XXXIX.

JANUARY 5th and 6th.—The whole scene made a deep impression on our minds, and Owen's speech coming as a sort of climax, brought before us our misery with a force that was well-nigh overwhelming.

As soon as I recovered my composure, I did not forget to thank Andre Letourneur for the act of intervention that had saved my life.

"Do you thank me for that; Mr. Kazallon?" he said; "it has only served to prolong your misery."

"Never mind, M. Letourneur," said Miss Herbey; "you did your duty."

Enfeebled and emaciated as the young girl is, her sense of duty never deserts her, and although her torn and bedraggled garments float dejectedly about her body, she never utters a word of complaint, and never loses courage.

"Mr. Kazallon," she said to me, "do you think we are fated to die of hunger?"

"Yes; Miss Herbey, I do," I replied in a hard, cold tone.

"How long do you suppose we have to live?" she asked again.

"I cannot say; perhaps we shall linger on longer than we imagine."

"The strongest constitutions suffer the most, do they not?" she said.

"Yes; but they have one consolation; they die the soonest;" I replied coldly.

Had every spark of humanity died out of my breast that I thus brought the girl face to face with the terrible truth without a word of hope or comfort? The eyes of Andre and his father, dilated with hunger, were fixed upon me, and I saw reproach and astonishment written in their faces.

Afterwards, when we were quite alone, Miss Herbey asked me if I would grant her a favour.

"Certainly, Miss Herbey; anything you like to ask," I replied; and this time my manner was kinder and more genial.

"Mr. Kazallon," she said, "I am weaker than you, and shall probably die first. Promise me that, if I do, you will throw my body into the sea."

"Oh, Miss Herbey," I began, "it was very wrong of me to speak to you as I did!"

"No, no," she replied, half smiling; "you were quite right. But it is a weakness of mine; I don't mind what they do with me as long as I am alive, but when I am dead—" she stopped and shuddered. "Oh, promise me that you will throw me into, the sea!"

I gave her the melancholy promise, which she acknowledged by pressing my hand feebly with her emaciated fingers.

Another night passed away. At times my sufferings were so intense that cries of agony involuntarily escaped my lips; then I became calmer, and sank into a kind of lethargy. When I awoke, I was surprised to find my companions still alive.

The one of our party who seems to bear his privations the best is Hobart the steward, a man with whom hitherto I have had very little to do. He is small, with a fawning expression remarkable for its indecision, and has a smile which is incessantly playing round his lips; he goes about with his eyes half-closed, as though he wished to conceal his thoughts, and there is something altogether false and hypocritical about his whole demeanour. I cannot say that he bears his privations without a murmur, for he sighs and moans incessantly; but, with it all, I cannot but think that there is a want of genuineness in his manner, and that the privation has not really told upon him as much as it has upon the rest of us. I have my suspicions about the man, and intend to watch him carefully. To-day, the 6th, M. Letourneur drew me aside to the stern of the raft, saying that he had a secret to communicate, but that he wished neither to be seen nor heard speaking to me. I withdrew with him to the larboard corner of the raft; and, as it was growing dusk, nobody observed what we were doing.

"Mr. Kazallon," M. Letourneur began in a low voice, "Andre is dying of hunger: he is growing weaker and weaker, and oh! I cannot, will not see him die!"

He spoke passionately, almost fiercely, and I fully understood his feelings. Taking his hand, I tried to reassure him.

"We will not despair yet," I said, "perhaps some passing ship—"

"Ship!" he cried impatiently, "don't try to console me with empty commonplaces; you know as well as I do that there is no chance of falling in with a passing ship." Then, breaking off suddenly, he asked,—"How long is it since my son and all of you have had anything to eat?"

Astonished at his question, I replied that it was now four days since the biscuit had failed.

"Four days," he repeated; "well, then, it is eight since I have tasted anything. I have been saving my share for my son."

Tears rushed to my eyes; for a few moments I was unable to speak, and could only once more grasp his hand in silence.

"What do you want me to do?" I asked at length.

"Hush! not so loud; some one will hear us," he said, lowering his voice, "I want you to offer it to Andre as though it came from yourself. He would not accept it from me; he would think I had been depriving myself for him. Let me implore you to do me this service and for your trouble," and here he gently stroked my hand, "for your trouble you shall have a morsel for yourself."

I trembled like a child as I listened to the poor father's words, and my heart was ready to burst when I felt a tiny piece of biscuit slipped into my hand.

"Give it him," M. Letourneur went on under his breath, "give it him; but do not let any one see you; the monsters would murder you if they knew it. This is only for to-day; I will give you some more to-morrow."

The poor fellow did not trust me, and well he might not, for I had the greatest difficulty to withstand the temptation to carry the biscuit to my mouth, But I resisted the impulse, and those alone who have suffered like me can know what the effort was.

Night came on with the rapidity peculiar to these low latitudes, and I glided gently up to Andre and slipped the piece of biscuit into his hand as "a present from myself." The young man clutched at it eagerly.

"But my father?" he said inquiringly.

I assured him that his father and I had each had our share, and that he must eat this now, and, perhaps, I should be able to bring him some more another time. Andre asked no more questions, and eagerly devoured the morsel of food.

So this evening at least, notwithstanding M. Letourneur's offer, I have tasted nothing.

CHAPTER XL.

JANUARY 7th.—During the last few days since the wind has freshened, the salt water constantly dashing over the raft has terribly punished the feet and legs of some of the sailors. Owen, whom the boatswain ever since the revolt kept bound to the mast, is in a deplorable state, and at our request has been released from his restraint. Sandon and Burke are also suffering from the severe smarting caused in this way, and it is only owing to our more sheltered position on the aft-part of the raft, that we have not; all shared the same inconvenience.

Today the boatswain, maddened by starvation, laid hands upon everything that met his voracious eyes, and I could hear the grating of his teeth as he gnawed at fragments of sails and bits of wood, instinctively endeavouring to fill his stomach by putting the mucus' into circulation at length, by dint of an eager search, he came upon a piece of leather hanging to one of the spars that supported the platform. He snatched it off and devoured it greedily, and as it was animal matter, it really seemed as though the absorption of the substance afforded him some temporary relief. Instantly we all followed his example; a leather hat, the rims of caps, in short, anything that contained any animal matter at all, were gnawed and sucked with the utmost avidity. Never shall I forget the scene. We were no longer human, the impulses and instincts of brute beasts seemed to actuate our every movement.

For a moment the pangs of hunger were somewhat allayed; but some of us revolted against the loathsome food, and were seized either with violent nausea or absolute sickness. I must be pardoned for giving these distressing details, but how otherwise can I depict the misery, moral and physical, which we are enduring? And with it all, I dare not venture to hope that we have reached the climax of our sufferings.

The conduct of Hobart during the scene that I have just described has only served to confirm my previous suspicions of him. He took no part in the almost fiendish energy with which we gnawed at our scraps of leather, and although by his conduct and perpetual groanings, he might be considered to be dying of inanition, yet to me he has the appearance of being singularly exempt from the tortures which we are all enduring. But whether the hypocrite is being sustained, by some secret store of food, I have been unable to discover.

Whenever the breeze drops the heat is overpowering; but although our allowance of water is very meagre, at present the pangs of hunger far exceed the pain of thirst. It has often been remarked that extreme thirst is far less endurable than extreme hunger. Is it possible that still greater agonies are in store for us? I cannot, dare not, believe it. Fortunately, the broken barrel still contains a few pints of water, and the other one has not yet been opened. But I am glad to say that notwithstanding our diminished numbers, and in spite of some opposition, the captain has thought right to reduce the daily allowance to half a pint for each person. As for the brandy, of which there is only a quart now left, it has been stowed away safely in the stern of the raft.

This evening has ended the sufferings of another of our companions, making our number now only fourteen. My attentions and Miss Herbey's nursing could do nothing for Lieutenant Walter, and about half-past seven he expired in my arms.

Before he died, in a few broken words he thanked Miss Herbey and myself for the kindness we had shown him. A crumpled letter fell from his hand, and in a voice that was scarcely audible from weakness, he said,—

"It is my mother's letter: the last I had from her—she was expecting me home; but she will never see me more. Oh, put it to my lips—let me kiss it before I die. Mother! mother! Oh my God!"

I placed the letter in his cold hand, and raised it to his lips; his eye lighted for a moment; we heard the faint sound of a kiss, and all was over!

CHAPTER XLI.

JANUARY 8th.—All night I remained by the side of the poor fellow's corpse, and several times Miss Herbey joined me in my mournful watch.

Before daylight dawned the body was quite cold, and as I knew there must be no delay in throwing it overboard, I asked Curtis to assist me in the sad office. The body was frightfully emaciated, and I had every hope that it would not float.

As soon as it was quite light, taking every precaution that no one should see what we were about, Curtis and I proceeded to our melancholy task. We took a few articles from the lieutenant's pockets, which we purposed, if either of us should survive, to remit to his mother. But as we wrapped him in his tattered garments that would have to suffice for his winding-sheet, I started back with a thrill of horror. The right foot had gone, leaving the leg a bleeding stump!

No doubt that, overcome by fatigue, I must have fallen asleep for an interval during the night, and some one had taken advantage of my slumber to mutilate the corpse. But who could have been guilty of so foul a deed! Curtis looked around with anger flashing In his eye; but all seemed as usual, and the silence was only broken by a few groans of agony.

But there was no time to be lost; perhaps we were already observed, and more horrible scenes might be likely to occur. Curtis said a few short prayers, and we cast the body into the sea. It sank immediately.

"They are feeding the sharks well, and no mistake," said a voice behind me.

I turned round quickly, and found that it was Jynxstrop who had spoken.

As the boatswain now approached, I asked him whether he thought it possible that any of the wretched men could have taken the dead man's foot.

"Oh yes, I dare say," he replied, in a significant tone "and perhaps they thought they were right."

"Right! what do you mean?" I exclaimed.

"Well, sir," he said coldly, "isn't it better to eat a dead man than a living one?"

I was at a loss to comprehend him, and, turning away, laid myself down at the end of the raft.

Towards eleven o'clock, a most suspicious incident occurred. The boatswain, who had cast his lines early in the morning, caught three large cod, each more than thirty inches long, of the species which, when dried, is known by the name of stock-fish. Scarcely had he hauled them on board, when the sailors made a dash at them, and it was with the utmost difficulty that Curtis, Falsten, and myself could restore order, so that we might divide the fish into equal portions. Three cod were not much amongst fourteen starving persons, but, small as the quantity was, it was allotted in strictly equal shares. Most of us devoured the food raw, almost I might say, alive; only Curtis, Andre and Miss Herbey having the patience to wait until their allowance had been boiled at a fire which they made with a few scraps of wood. For myself, I confess that I swallowed my portion of fish just as it was,—raw and bleeding. M. Letourneur followed my example; the poor man devoured his food like a famished wolf, and it is only a wonder to me how, after his lengthened fast, he came to be alive at all.

The boatswain's delight at his success was, excessive, and amounted almost to delirium. I went up to him, and encouraged him to repeat his attempt.

"Oh, yes," he said; "I'll try again. I'll try again."

"And why not try at once," I asked.

"Not now," he said evasively; "the night is the best time for catching large fish. Besides, I must manage to get some bait, for we have been improvident enough not to save a single scrap."

"But you have succeeded once without bait; why may you not succeed again?"

"Oh! I had some very good bait last night," he said. I stared at him in amazement. He steadily returned my gaze, but said nothing.

"Have you none left?" at last I asked.

"Yes!" he almost whispered and left me without another word.

Our meal, meagre as it had been, served to rally our shattered energies; our hopes were slightly raised; there was no reason why the boatswain should not have the same good luck again.

One evidence of the degree to which our spirits were revived was that our minds were no longer fixed upon the miserable present and hopeless future, but we began to recall and discuss the past; and M. Letourneur, Andre Mr. Falsten, and I held a long conversation with the captain about the various incidents of our eventful voyage, speaking of our lost companions, of the fire, of the stranding of the ship, of our sojourn on

Ham Rock, of the springing of the leak, of our terrible voyage in the topmasts, of the construction of the raft, and of the storm. All these things seemed to have happened so long ago, and yet we were living still. Living, did I say? Ay, if such an existence as ours could be called a life, fourteen of us were living still. Who would be the next to go? We should then be thirteen.

"An unlucky number!" said Andre with a mournful smile.

During the night the boatswain cast his lines from the stern of the raft, and, unwilling to trust them to any one else, remained watching them himself. In the morning I went to ascertain what success had attended his patience. It was scarcely light, and with eager eyes he was peering down into the water. He had neither seen nor heard me coming.

"Well, boatswain!" I said, touching him on the shoulder.

He turned round quickly.

"Those villainous sharks have eaten every morsel of my bait," he said, in a desponding voice.

"And you have no more left?" I asked.

"No more," he said. Then grasping my arm he added, "and that only shows me that it is no good doing things by halves."

The truth flashed upon me at once, and I laid my hand upon his mouth. Poor Walter!

CHAPTER XLII.

JANUARY 9th and 10th.—On the 9th the wind dropped, and there was a dead calm; not a ripple disturbed the surface of the long undulations as they rose and fell beneath us; and if it were not for the slight current which is carrying us we know not whither, the raft would be absolutely stationary.

The heat was intolerable; our thirst more intolerable still; and now it was that for the first time I fully realized how the insufficiency of drink could cause torture more unendurable than the pangs of hunger. Mouth, throat, pharynx, all alike were parched and dry, every gland becoming hard as horn under the action of the hot air we breathed. At my urgent solicitation the captain was for once induced to double our allowance of water; and this relaxation of the ordinary rule enabled us to attempt to slake our thirst four times in the day, instead of only twice. I use the word "attempt" advisedly; for the water at the bottom of the barrel, though kept covered by a sail, became so warm that it was perfectly flat and unrefreshing.

It was a most trying day, and the sailors relapsed into a condition of deep despondency. The moon was nearly full, but when she rose the breeze did not return. Continuance of high temperature in daytime is a sure proof that we have been carried far to the south, and here, on this illimitable ocean, we have long ceased even to look for land; it might almost seem as though this globe of ours had veritably become a liquid sphere!

To-day we are still becalmed, and the temperature is as high as ever. The air is heated like a furnace, and the sun scorches like fire. The torments of famine are all forgotten: our thoughts are concentrated with fevered expectation upon the longed-for moment when Curtis shall dole out the scanty measure of lukewarm water that makes up our ration. O for one good draught, even if it should exhaust the whole supply! At least, it seems as if we then could die in peace!

About noon we were startled by sharp cries of agony, and looking round I saw Owen writhing in the most horrible convulsions. I went towards him, for, detestable as his conduct had been, common humanity prompted me to see whether I could afford him any relief. But before I reached him, a shout from Flaypole arrested my attention.

The man was up in the mast, and with great excitement pointing to the east.

"A ship! A ship!" he cried.

In an instant all were on their feet. Even Owen stopped his cries and stood erect. It was quite true that in the direction indicated by Flaypole there was a white speck visible upon the horizon. But did it move? Would the sailors with their keen vision pronounce it to be a sail? A silence the most profound fell upon us all. I glanced at Curtis as he stood with folded arms intently gazing at the distant point. His brow was furrowed, and he contracted every feature, as with half-closed eyes, he concentrated his power of vision upon that one faint spot in the far-off horizon.

But at length he dropped his arms and shook his head. I looked again, but the spot was no longer there. If it were a ship, that ship had disappeared; but probably it had been a mere reflection, or, more likely still, only the crest of some curling wave.

A deep dejection followed this phantom ray of hope. All returned to their accustomed places. Curtis alone remained motionless, but his eye no longer scanned the distant view.

Owen now began to shriek more wildly than ever. He presented truly a most melancholy sight; he writhed with the most hideous contortions, and had all the appearance of suffering from tetanus. His throat was contracted by repeated spasms, his tongue was parched, his body swollen, and his pulse, though feeble, was rapid and irregular. The poor wretch's symptoms were precisely such as to lead us to suspect that he had taken some corrosive poison. Of course it was quite out of our power to administer any antidote; all that we could devise was to make him swallow something that might act as an emetic. I asked Curtis for a little of the lukewarm water. As the contents of the broken barrel were now exhausted, the captain, in order to comply with my request, was about to tap the other barrel, when Owen started suddenly to his knees, and with a wild, unearthly shriek, exclaimed,—

"No! no! no! of that water I will not touch a drop."

I supposed he did not understand what we were going to do, and endeavoured to explain; but all in vain; he persisted in refusing to taste the water in the second barrel. I then tried to induce vomiting by tickling his uvula, and he brought off some bluish secretion from his stomach, the character of which confirmed our previous suspicions—that he had been poisoned by oxide of copper. We now felt convinced that any efforts on our part to save him would be of no avail. The vomiting, however, had for the time relieved him, and he was able to speak.

Curtis and I both implored him to let us know what he had taken to bring about consequences so serious. His reply fell upon us as a startling blow.

The ill fated wretch had stolen several pints of water from the barrel that had been untouched, and that water had poisoned him!

CHAPTER XLIII.

JANUARY 11th to 14th.—Owen's convulsions returned with increased violence, and in the course of the night he expired in terrible agony. His body was thrown overboard almost directly; it had decomposed so rapidly that the flesh had not even consistency enough for any fragments of it to be reserved for the boatswain to use to bait his lines. A plague the man had been to us in his life; in his death he was now of no service!

And now, perhaps, still more than ever, did the horror of our situation stare us in the face. There was no doubt that the poisoned barrel had at some time or other contained copperas; but what strange fatality had converted it into a water-cask, or what fatality, stranger still, had caused it to be brought on board the raft, was a problem that none could solve. Little, however, did it matter now: the fact was evident; the barrel was poisoned, and of water we had not a drop.

One and all, we fell into the gloomiest silence. We were too irritable to bear the sound of each other's voices; and it did not require a word, a mere look or gesture was enough, to provoke us to anger that was little short of madness. How it was that we did not all become raving maniacs, I cannot tell.

Throughout the 12th no drain of moisture crossed our lips, and not a cloud arose to warrant the expectation of a passing shower; in the shade, if shade it might be called, the thermometer would have registered at least 100deg., and, perhaps, considerably more.

No change next day. The salt water began to chafe my legs, but although the smarting was at times severe, it was an inconvenience to which I gave little heed; others who had suffered from the same trouble had become no worse. Oh! if this water that surrounds us could be reduced to vapour or to ice! its particles of salt extracted, it would be available for drink. But no! we have no appliances, and we must suffer on.

At the risk of being devoured by the sharks, the boatswain and two sailors took a morning bath, and as their plunge seemed to refresh them, I and three of my companions resolved to follow their example. We had never learnt to swim, and had to be fastened to the end of a rope and lowered into the water; while Curtis during the half-hour of our bath, kept a sharp look-out to give warning of any danger from approaching sharks. No recommendation, however, on our part, nor any representation of the benefit we felt we had derived, could induce Miss Herbey to allay her sufferings in the same way.

At about eleven o'clock, the captain came up to me, and whispered in my ear,—

"Don't say a word, Mr. Kazallon; I do not want to raise false hopes, but I think I see a ship."

It was as well that the captain had warned me; otherwise, I should have raised an involuntary shout of joy; as it was, I had the greatest difficulty in restraining my expressions of delight.

"Look behind to larboard," he continued in an undertone.

Affecting an indifference which I was far from feeling, I cast an anxious glance to that quarter of the horizon of which he spoke, and there, although mine is not a nautical eye, I could plainly distinguish the outline of a ship under sail.

Almost at the same moment the boatswain who happened to be looking in the same direction, raised the cry, "Ship ahoy!"

Whether it was that no one believed it, or whether all energies were exhausted, certain it is that the announcement produced none of the effects that might have been expected. Not a soul exhibited the slightest emotion, and it was only when the boatswain had several times sung out his tidings that all eyes turned to the horizon. There, most undeniably, was the ship, and the question rose at once to the minds of all, and to the lips of many, "Would she see us?"

The sailors immediately began discussing the build of the vessel, and made all sorts of conjectures as to the direction she was taking. Curtis was far more deliberate in his judgment. After examining her attentively for some time, he said, "She is a brig running close upon the wind, on the starboard tack, If she keeps her course for a couple of hours, she will come right athwart our track."

A couple of hours! The words sounded to our ears like a couple of centuries. The ship might change her course at any moment; closely trimmed as she was, it was very probable that she was only tacking about to catch the wind, in which case, as soon as she felt a breeze, she would resume her larboard tack and make away again. On the other hand, if she were really sailing with the wind, she would come nearer to us, and there would be good ground for hope.

Meantime, no exertion must be spared, and no means left untried, to make our position known. The brig was about twelve miles to the east of us, so that it was out of the question to think of any cries of ours being overheard; but Curtis gave directions that every possible signal should be made. We had no fire-arms by which we could attract attention, and nothing else occurred to us beyond hoisting a flag of distress. Miss Herbey's red shawl, as being of a colour most distinguishable against the background of sea and sky, was run up to the mast-head, and was caught by the light breeze that just then was ruffling the surface of the water. As a drowning man clutches at a straw, so our hearts bounded with hope every time that our poor flag fluttered in the wind.

For an hour our feelings alternated between hope and despair. The ship was evidently making her way in the direction of the raft, but every now and then she seemed to stop, and then our hearts would almost stand still with agony lest she was going to put about. She carried all her canvas, even to her royals and stay-sails, but her hull was only partially visible above the horizon.

How slowly she advanced! The breeze was very, very feeble, and perhaps soon it would drop altogether! We felt that we would give years of our life to know the result of the coming hour!

At half-past twelve the captain and the boatswain considered that the brig was about nine miles away; she had, therefore, gained only three miles in an hour and a half, and it was doubtful whether the light breeze that had been passing over our heads had reached her at all. I fancied, too, that her sails were no longer filled, but were hanging loose against her masts. Turning to the direction of the wind I tried to make out some chance of a rising breeze; but no, the waves were calm and torpid, and the little puff of air that had aroused our hopes had died away across the sea.

I stood aft with M. Letourneur, Andre and Miss Herbey, and our glances perpetually wandered from the distant ship to our captain's face. Curtis stood leaning against the mast, with the boatswain by his side; their eyes seemed never for a moment to cease to watch the brig, but their countenances clearly expressed the varying emotions that passed through their minds. Not a word was uttered, nor was the silence broken, until the carpenter exclaimed, in accents of despair,—

"She's putting about!"

All started up: some to their knees, others to their feet, The boatswain dropped a frightful oath. The ship was still nine miles away, and at such a distance it was impossible for our signal to be seen; our tiny raft, a mere speck upon the waters, would be lost in the intense irradiation of the sunbeams. If only we could be seen, no doubt all would be well; no captain would have the barbarous inhumanity to leave us to our fate; but there had been no chance; only too well we knew that we had not been within the range of sight.

"My friends," said Curtis, "we must make a fire; it is our last and only chance."

Some planks were quickly loosened and thrown into a heap upon the fore part of the raft. They were damp and troublesome to light; but the very dampness made the smoke more dense, and ere long a tall column of dusky fumes was rising straight upwards in the air. If darkness should come on before the brig was completely out of view, the flames we hoped might still be visible. But the hours passed on; the fire died out; and yet no signs of help.

The temper of resignation now deserted me entirely; faith, hope, confidence—all vanished from my mind, and like the boatswain, I swore long and loudly. A gentle hand was laid upon my arm, and turning round I saw Miss Herbey with her finger pointing to the sky. I could stand it no longer, but gliding underneath the tent I hid my face in my hands and wept aloud.

Meanwhile the brig had altered her tack, and was moving slowly to the east. Three hours later and the keenest eye could not have discerned her top-sails above the horizon.

CHAPTER XLIV.

JANUARY 15th.—After this further shattering of our excited hopes death alone now stares us in the face; slow and lingering as that death may be, sooner or later it must inevitably come.

To-day some clouds that rose in the west have brought us a few puffs of wind; and in spite of our prostration, we appreciate the moderation, slight as it is, in the temperature. To my parched throat the air seemed a little less trying but it is now seven days since the boatswain took his haul of fish, and during that period we have eaten nothing even Andre Letourneur finished yesterday the last morsel of the biscuit which his sorrowful and self-denying father had entrusted to my charge.

Jynxstrop the negro has broken loose from his confinement, but Curtis has taken no measures for putting him again under restraint. It is not to be apprehended that the miserable fellow and his accomplices, weakened as they are by their protracted fast, will attempt to do us any mischief now.

Some huge sharks made their appearance to-day, cleaving the water rapidly with their great black fins. The monsters came close up to the edge of the raft, and Flaypole, who was leaning over, narrowly escaped having his arm snapped off by one of them. I could not help regarding them as living sepulchres, which ere long might swallow up our miserable carcasses; yet, withal, I profess that my feelings were rather those of fascination than of horror.

The boatswain, who stood with clenched teeth and dilated eye, regarded these sharks from quite another point of view. He thought about devouring the sharks, not about the sharks devouring him; and if he could succeed in catching one, I doubt if one of us would reject the tough and untempting flesh. He determined to make the attempt, and as he had no whirl which he could fasten to his rope he set to work to find something that might serve as a substitute. Curtis and Dowlas were consulted, and after a short conversation, during which they kept throwing bits of rope and spars into the water in order to entice the sharks to remain by the raft, Dowlas went and fetched his carpenter's tool, which is at once a hatchet and a hammer. Of this he proposed to make the whirl of which they were in need, under the hope that either the sharp edge of the adze or the pointed extremity opposite would stick firmly into the jaws of any shark that might swallow it. The wooden handle of the hammer was secured to the rope, which, in its turn, was tightly fastened to the raft.

With eager, almost breathless, excitement we stood watching the preparations, at the same time using every means in our power to attract the attention of the sharks. As soon as the whirl was ready the boatswain began to think about bait; and, talking rapidly to himself, ransacked every corner of the raft, as though he expected to find some dead body coming opportunely to sight. But his search ended in nothing; and the only plan that suggested itself was again to have recourse to Miss Herbey's red shawl, of which a fragment was wrapped round the head of the hammer. After testing the strength of his line, and reassuring-himself that it was fastened firmly both to the hammer and to the raft, the boatswain lowered it into the water.

The sea was quite transparent, and any object was clearly visible to a depth of two hundred feet below the surface. Leaning over the low parapet of the raft we looked on in breathless silence, as the scarlet rag, distinct as it was against the blue mass of water, made its slow descent. But one by one the sharks seemed to disappear, They could not, however, have gone far away, and it was not likely that anything in the shape of bait dropped near them would long escape their keen voracity.

Suddenly, without speaking, the boatswain raised his hand and pointed to a dark mass skimming along the surface of the water, and making straight in our direction. It was a shark, certainly not less than twelve feet long. As soon as the creature was about four fathoms from the raft, the boatswain gently drew in his line until the whirl was in such a position that the shark must cross right over it; at the same time he shook the line a little, that he might give the whirl the appearance, if he could, of being something alive and moving. As the creature came near, my heart beat violently; I could see its eyes flashing above the waves; and its gaping jaws, as it turned half over on its back, exhibited long rows of pointed teeth.

I know not who it was, but some one at that moment uttered an involuntary cry of horror. The shark came to a standstill, turned about, and escaped quite out of sight. The boatswain was pale with anger.

"The first man who speaks," he said, "I will kill him on the spot."

Again he applied himself to his task. The whirl again was lowered, this time to the depth of twenty fathoms, but for half an hour or more not a shark could be distinguished; but as the waters far below seemed somehow to be troubled I could not help believing that some of the brutes at least were still there.

All at once, with a violent jerk, the cord was wrested from the boatswain's hands; firmly attached, however, as it was to the raft, it was not lost. The bait had been seized by a shark, and the iron had made good its hold upon the creature's flesh.

"Now, then, my lads," cried the boatswain, "haul away!"

Passengers and sailors, one and all, put forth what strength they had to drag the rope, but so violent were the creature's struggles that it required all our efforts (and it is needless to say that they were willing enough) to bring it to the surface, At length, after exertions that almost exhausted us, the water became agitated by the violent flappings of the tail and fins; and looking down I saw the huge carcase of the shark writhing convulsively amidst waves that were stained with blood.

"Steady! steady!" said the boatswain, as the head appeared above.

The whirl had passed right through the jaw into the middle of the throat; so that no struggle on the part of the animal could possibly release it. Dowlas seized his hatchet, ready to despatch the brute the moment if should be landed on the raft. A short sharp snap was heard. The shark had closed its jaws, and bitten through the wooden handle of the hammer. Another moment and it had turned round and was completely gone.

A howl of despair burst from all our lips. All the labour and the patience, all had been in vain. Dowlas made a few more unsuccessful attempts, but as the whirl was lost, and they had no means of replacing it, there was no further room for hope. They did, indeed, lower some cords twisted into running knots, but (as might have been expected) these only slipped over, without holding, the slimy bodies of the sharks. As a last resource the boatswain allowed his naked leg to hang over the side of the raft; the monsters, however, were proof even against this attraction.

Reduced once again to a gloomy despondency, all turned to their places, to await the end that cannot now be long deferred.

Just as I moved away I heard the boatswain say to Curtis,—

"Captain, when shall we draw lots?"

The captain made no reply.

CHAPTER XLV.

JANUARY 16th.—If the crew of any passing vessel had caught sight of us as we lay still and inanimate upon our sail-cloth, they would scarcely, at first sight, have hesitated to pronounce us dead.

My sufferings were terrible; tongue, lips, and throat were so parched and swollen that if food had been at hand I question whether I could have swallowed it. So exasperated were the feelings of us all, however, that we glanced at each other with looks as savage as though we were about to slaughter and without delay eat up one another.

The heat was aggravated by the atmosphere being somewhat stormy. Heavy vapours gathered on the horizon, and there was a look as if it were raining all around. Longing eyes and gasping mouths turned involuntarily towards the clouds, and M. Letourneur, on bended knee, was raising his hands, as it might be in supplication to the relentless skies.

It was eleven o'clock in the morning. I listened for distant rumblings which might announce an approaching storm, but although the vapours had obstructed the sun's rays, they no longer presented the appearance of being charged with electricity. Thus our prognostications ended in disappointment; the clouds, which in the early morning had been marked by the distinctness of their outline, had melted one into another and assumed an uniform dull grey tint; in fact, we were enveloped in an ordinary fog. But was it not still possible that this fog might turn to rain?

Happily this hope was destined to be realized; for in a very short time, Dowlas, with a shout of delight, declared that rain was actually coming; and sure enough, not half a mile from the raft, the dark parallel streaks against the sky testified that there at least the rain was falling. I fancied I could see the drops rebounding from the surface of the water. The wind was fresh and bringing the cloud right on towards us, yet we could not suppress our trepidation lest it; should exhaust itself before it reached us.

But no: very soon large heavy drops began to fall, and the storm-cloud, passing over our heads, was outpouring its contents upon us. The shower, however, was very transient; already a bright streak of light along the horizon marked the limit of the cloud and warned us that we must be quick to make the most of what it had to give us. Curtis had placed the broken barrel in the position that was most exposed, and every sail was spread out to the fullest extent our dimensions would allow.

We all laid ourselves down flat upon our backs and kept our mouths wide open. The rain splashed into my face, wetted my lips, and trickled down my throat. Never can I describe the ecstasy with which I imbibed that renovating moisture. The parched and swollen glands relaxed, I breathed afresh, and my whole being seemed revived with a strange and requickened life.

The rain lasted about twenty minutes, when the cloud, still only half exhausted, passed quite away from over us.

We grasped each other's hands as we rose from the platform on which we had been lying, and mutual congratulations, mingled with gratitude, poured forth from our long silent lips. Hope, however evanescent it might be, for the moment had returned, and we yielded to the expectation that, ere long, other and more abundant clouds might come and replenish our store.

The next consideration was how to preserve and economize what little had been collected by the barrel, or imbibed by the outspread sails. It was found that only a few pints of rain-water had fallen into the barrel to this small quantity the sailors were about to add what they could by wringing out the saturated sails, when Curtis made them desist from their intention.

"Stop, stop!" he said, "we must wait a moment; we must see whether this water from the sails is drinkable."

I looked at him in amazement. Why should not this be as drinkable as the other? He squeezed a few drops out of one of the folds of a sail into the tin pot, and put it to his lips. To my surprise, he rejected it immediately, and upon tasting it for myself I found it not merely brackish, but briny as the sea itself. The fact was that the canvas had been so long exposed to the action of the waves, that it had become thoroughly impregnated by salt, which of course was taken up again by the water that fell upon it. Disappointed we were; but with several pints of water in our possession, we were not only contented for the present, but sanguine in our prospect for the future.

CHAPTER XLVI.

JANUARY 17th.—As a natural consequence of the alleviation of our thirst, the pangs of hunger returned more violently than ever. Although we had no bait, and even if we had we could not use it for want of a whirl, we could not help asking whether no possible means could be devised for securing one out of the many sharks that were still perpetually swarming about the raft. Armed with knives, like the Indians in the pearl fisheries, was it not practicable to attack the monsters in their own element? Curtis expressed his willingness personally to make the attempt, but so numerous were the sharks that we would not for one moment hear of his risking his life in a venture of which the danger was as great as the success was doubtful.

By plunging into the sea, or by gnawing at a piece of metal, we could always, or at least often, do something that cheated us into believing that we were mitigating the pains of thirst; but with hunger it was different. The prospect, too, of rain seemed hopeful, whilst for getting food there appeared no chance; and, as we knew that nothing could compensate for the lack of nutritive matter, we were soon all cast down again. Shocking to confess, it would be untrue to deny that we surveyed each other with the eye of an eager longing; and I need hardly explain to what a degree of savageness the one idea that haunted us had reduced our feelings.

Ever since the storm-cloud brought us the too transient shower the sky has been tolerably clear, and although at that time the wind had slightly freshened, it has since dropped, and the sail hangs idly against our mast. Except for the trifling relief it brings by modifying the temperature we care little now for any breeze. Ignorant as we are as to what quarter of the Atlantic we have been carried by the currents, it matters very little to us from what direction the wind may blow if only it would bring, in rain or dew, the moisture of which we are so dreadfully in need.

The moon was entering her last quarter, so that it was dark till nearly midnight, and the stars were misty, not glowing with that lustre which is so often characteristic of cool nights. Half frantic with that sense of hunger which invariably returns with redoubled vigour at the close of every day, I threw myself, in a kind of frenzy, upon a bundle of sails that was lying on the starboard of the raft, and leaning over, I tried to get some measure of relief by inhaling the moist coolness that rarely fails to circulate just above the water. My brain was haunted by the most horrible nightmares; not that I suppose I was in any way more distressed than my companions, who were lying in their usual places, vainly endeavouring to forget their sufferings in sleep.

After a time I fell into a restless, dreamy doze. I was neither asleep nor awake. How long I remained in that state of stupor I could hardly say, but at length a strange sensation half brought me to myself. Was I dreaming, or was there not really some unaccustomed odour floating in the air? My nostrils became distended, and I could scarcely suppress a cry of astonishment; but some instinct kept me quiet, and I laid myself down again with the puzzled sensation sometimes experienced when we have forgotten a word or name. Only a few minutes, however, had elapsed before another still more savoury puff induced me to take several long inhalations. Suddenly, the truth seemed to dash across my mind. "Surely," I muttered to myself "this must be cooked meat that I can smell."

Again and again I sniffed and became more convinced than ever that my senses were not deceiving me. But from what part of the raft could the smell proceed? I rose to my knees, and having satisfied myself that the odour came from the front, I crept stealthily as a cat under the sails and between the spars in that direction. Following the promptings of my scent, rather than my vision, like a bloodhound in the track of his prey, I searched everywhere I could, now finding, now losing, the smell according to my change of position, or the dropping of the wind. At length I got the true scent; once for all, so that I could go straight to the object for which I was in search.

Approaching the starboard angle of the raft, I came to the conclusion that the smell that had thus keenly excited my cravings was the smell of smoked bacon; the membranes of my tongue almost bristled with the intenseness of my longing.

Crawling along a little farther, under a thick roll of sail-cloth, I was not long in securing my prize. Forcing my arm below the roll, I felt my hand in contact with something wrapped up in paper. I clutched it up, and carried it off to a place where I could examine it by the help of the light of the moon that had now made its appearance above the horizon. I almost shrieked for joy. It was a piece of bacon. True, it did not weigh many ounces, but small as it was it would suffice to alleviate the pangs of hunger for one day at least. I was just on the point of raising it to my mouth, when a hand was laid upon my arm. It was only by a most determined effort that I kept myself from screaming out one instant more, and I found myself face to face with Hobart.

In a moment I understood all. Plainly this rascal Hobart had saved some provision from the wreck, upon which he had been subsisting ever since. The steward had provided for himself, whilst all around him were dying of starvation. Detestable wretch! This accounts for the inconsistency of his well-to-do looks and his pitiable groans. Vile hypocrite!

Yet why, it struck me, should I complain? Was not I reaping the benefit of that secret store that he, for himself, had saved?

But Hobart had no idea of allowing me the peaceable possession of what he held to be his own. He made a dash at the fragment of bacon, and seemed determined to wrest it from my grasp. We struggled with each other, but although our wrestling was very violent, it was very noiseless. We were both of us aware that it was absolutely necessary that not one of those on board should know anything at all about the prize for which we were contending. Nor was my own determination lessened by hearing him groan out that it was his last, his only morsel. "His!" I thought; "it shall be mine now!"

And still careful that no noise of commotion should arise, I threw him on his back, and grasping his throat so that it gurgled again, I held him down until, in rapid mouthfuls, I had swallowed up the last scrap of the food for which we had fought so hard.

I released my prisoner, and quietly crept back to my own quarters.

And not a soul is aware that I have broken my fast!

CHAPTER XLVII.

JANUARY 18th.—After this excitement I awaited the approach of day with a strange anxiety. My conscience told me that Hobart had the right to denounce me in the presence of all my fellow-passengers; yet my alarm was vain. The idea of my proceedings being exposed by him was quite absurd; in a moment he would himself be murdered without pity by the crew, if it should be revealed that, unknown to them, he had been living on some private store which, by clandestine cunning, he had reserved. But, in spite of my anxiety, I had a longing for day to come.

The bit of food that I had thus stolen was very small; but small as it was it had alleviated my hunger, and I was now tortured with remorse, because I had not shared the meagre morsel with my fellow-sufferers. Miss Herbey, Andre, his father, all had been forgotten, and from the bottom of my heart I repented of my cruel selfishness.

Meantime the moon rose high in the heavens, and the first streaks of dawn appeared. There is no twilight in these low latitudes, and the full daylight came well nigh at once. I had not closed my eyes since my encounter with the steward, and ever since the first blush of day I had laboured under the impression that I could see some unusual dark mass half way up the mast. But although it again and again caught my eye, it hardly roused my curiosity, and I did not rise from the bundle of sails on which I was lying to ascertain what it really was. But no sooner did the rays of the sun fall full upon it than I saw at once that it was the body of a man, attached to a rope, and swinging to and fro with the motion of the raft.

A horrible presentiment carried me to the foot of the mast, and, just as I had guessed, Hobart had hanged himself. I could not for a moment; doubt that it was I myself that had impelled him to the suicide. A cry of horror had scarcely escaped my lips, when my fellow-passengers were at my side, and the rope was cut. Then came the sailors. And what was it that made the group gather so eagerly around the body? Was it a humane desire to see whether any spark of life remained? No, indeed; the corpse was cold, and the limbs were rigid; there was no chance that animation should be restored. What then was it that kept them lingering so close around? It was only too apparent what they were about to do.

But I did not, could not, look. I refused to take part in the horrible repast that was proposed. Neither would Miss Herbey, Andre nor his father, consent to alleviate their pangs of hunger by such revolting means. I know nothing for certain as to what Curtis did, and I did not venture to inquire; but of the others,—Falsten, Dowlas, the boatswain, and all the rest,—I know that, to assuage their cravings, they consented to reduce themselves to the level of beasts of prey; they were transformed from human beings into ravenous brutes.

The four of us who sickened at the idea of partaking of the horrid meal withdrew to the seclusion of our tent; it was bad enough to hear; without witnessing the appalling operation. But, in truth, I had the greatest difficulty in the world in preventing Andre from rushing out upon the cannibals, and snatching the odious food from their clutches. I represented to him the hopelessness of his attempt, and tried to reconcile him by telling him that if they liked the food they had a right to it. Hobart had not been murdered; he had died by his own hand; and, after all, as the boatswain had once remarked to me, "it was better to eat a dead man than a live one."

Do what I would, however, I could not quiet Andre's feeling of abhorrence; in his disgust and loathing he seemed for the time to have quite forgotten his own sufferings.

Meanwhile, there was no concealing the truth that we were ourselves dying of starvation, whilst our eight companions would probably, by their loathsome diet, escape that frightful destiny. Owing to his secret hoard of provisions Hobart had been by far the strongest amongst us; he had been supported, so that no organic disease had affected his tissues, and really might be said to be in good health when his chagrin drove him to his desperate suicide. But what was I thinking of! whither were my meditations carrying me away? was it not coming to pass that the cannibals were rousing my envy instead of exciting my horror?

Very shortly after this I heard Dowlas talking about the possibility of obtaining salt by evaporating sea-water in the sun; "and then," he added, "we can salt down the rest."

The boatswain assented to what the carpenter had said, and probably the suggestion was adopted.

Silence, the most profound, now reigns upon the raft. I presume that nearly all have gone to sleep. One thing I do know, that they are no longer hungry!

CHAPTER XLVIII.

JANUARY 19th.—All through the day the sky remained unclouded and the heat intense; and night came on without bringing much sensible moderation in the temperature. I was unable to get any sleep, and, towards morning, was disturbed by hearing an angry clamour going on outside the tent; it aroused M. Letourneur, Andre and Miss Herbey, as much as myself, and we were anxious to ascertain the cause of the tumult.

The boatswain, Dowlas, and all the sailors were storming at each other in frightful rage; and Curtis, who had come forward from the stern, was vainly endeavouring to pacify them.

"But who has done it? we must know who has done it," said Dowlas, scowling with vindictive passion on the group around him.

"There's a thief," howled out the boatswain, "and he shall be found! Let's know who has taken it."

"I haven't taken it!" "Nor I!" "Nor I!" cried the sailors one after another.

And then they set to work again to ransack every quarter of the raft; they rolled every spar aside, they overturned everything on board, and only grew more and more incensed with anger as their search proved fruitless.

"Can YOU tell us," said the boatswain, coming up to me, "who is the thief?"

"Thief!" I replied. "I don't know what you mean."

And while we were speaking the others all came up together, and told me that they had looked everywhere else, and that they were going now to search the tent.

"Shame!" I said. "You ought to allow those whom you know to be dying of hunger at least to die in peace. There is not one of us who has left the tent all night. Why suspect us?"

"Now just look here, Mr. Kazallon," said the boatswain, in a voice which he was endeavouring to calm down into moderation, "we are not accusing you of anything; we know well enough you, and all the rest of you, had a right to your shares as much as anybody; but that isn't it. It's all gone somewhere, every bit."

"Yes," said Sandon gruffly; "it's all gone somewheres, and we are a going to search the tent."

Resistance was useless, and Miss Herbey, M. Letourneur, and Andre were all turned out.

I confess I was very fearful. I had a strong suspicion that for the sake of his son, for whom he was ready to venture anything, M. Letourneur had committed the theft; in that case I knew that nothing would have prevented the infuriated men from tearing the devoted father to pieces. I beckoned to Curtis for protection, and he came and stood beside me. He said nothing, but waited with his hands in his pockets, and I think I am not mistaken in my belief that there was some sort of a weapon in each.

To my great relief the search was ineffectual. There was no doubt that the carcase of the suicide had been thrown overboard, and the rage of the disappointed cannibals knew no bounds.

Yet who had ventured to do the deed! I looked at M. Letourneur and Miss Herbey; but their countenances at once betrayed their ignorance. Andre turned his face away, and his eyes did not meet my own. Probably it is he; but, if it be, I wonder whether he has reckoned up the consequences of so rash an act.

CHAPTER XLIX.

JANUARY 20th to 22nd.—For the day or two after the horrible repast of the 18th those who had partaken of it appeared to suffer comparatively little either from hunger or thirst; but for the four of us who had tasted nothing, the agony of suffering grew more and more intense. It was enough to make us repine over the loss of the provision that had so mysteriously gone; and if any one of us should die, I doubt whether the survivors would a second time resist the temptation to assuage their pangs by tasting human flesh.

Before long, all the cravings of hunger began to return to the sailors, and I could see their eyes greedily glancing upon us, starved as they knew us to be, as though they were reckoning our hours, and already were preparing to consume us as their prey.

As is always the case with shipwrecked men, we were tormented by thirst far more than by hunger; and if, in the height of our sufferings, we had been offered our choice between a few drops of water and a few crumbs of biscuit, I do not doubt that we should, without exception, have preferred to take the water.

And what a mockery to our condition did it seem that all this while there was water, water, nothing but water, everywhere around us! Again and again, incapable of comprehending how powerless it was to relieve me, I put a few drops within my lips, but only with the invariable result of bringing on a most trying nausea, and rendering my thirst more unendurable than before.

Forty-two days had passed since we quitted the sinking "Chancellor." There could be no hope now; all of us must die, and by the most deplorable of deaths. I was quite conscious that a mist was gathering over my brain; I felt my senses sinking into a condition of torpor; I made an effort, but all in vain, to master the delirium that I was aware was taking possession of my reason. It is out of my power to decide for how long I lost my consciousness; but when I came to myself I found that Miss Herbey had folded some wet bandages around my forehead. I am somewhat better; but I am weakened, mind and body, and I am conscious that I have not long to live.

A frightful fatality occurred to-day. The scene was terrible. Jynxstrop the negro went raving mad. Curtis and several of the men tried their utmost to control him, but in spite of everything he broke loose, and tore up and down the raft, uttering fearful yells. He had gained possession of a handspike, and rushed upon us all with the ferocity of an infuriated tiger; how we contrived to escape mischief from his attacks, I know not. All at once, by one of those unaccountable impulses of madness, his rage turned against himself. With his teeth and nails he gnawed and tore away at his own flesh; dashing the blood into our faces, he shrieked out with a demoniacal grin, "Drink, drink!" and flinging us gory morsels, kept saying "Eat, eat!" In the midst of his insane shrieks he made a sudden pause, then dashing back again from the stern to the front, he made a bound and disappeared beneath the waves.

Falsten, Dowlas, and the boatswain, made a rush that at least they might secure the body; but it was too late; all that they could see was a crimson circle in the water, and some huge sharks disporting themselves around the spot.

CHAPTER L.

JANUARY 23rd.—Only eleven of us now remain; and the probability is very great that every day must now carry off at least its one victim, and perhaps more. The end of the tragedy is rapidly approaching, and save for the chance, which is next to an impossibility, of our sighting land, or being picked up by a passing vessel, ere another week has elapsed not a single survivor of the "Chancellor" will remain.

The wind freshened considerably in the night, and it is now blowing pretty briskly from the north-east. It has filled our sail, and the white foam in our wake is an indication that we are making some progress. The captain reckons that we must be advancing at the rate of about three miles an hour.

Curtis and Falsten are certainly in the best condition amongst us, and in spite of their extreme emaciation they bear up wonderfully under the protracted hardships we have all endured. Words cannot describe the melancholy state to which poor Miss Herbey bodily is reduced; her whole being seems absorbed into her soul, but that soul is brave and resolute as ever, living in heaven rather than on earth. The boatswain, strong, energetic man that he was, has shrunk into a mere shadow of his former self, and I doubt whether any one would recognize him to be the same man. He keeps perpetually to one corner of the raft, his head dropped upon his chest, and his long, bony hands lying upon knees that project sharply from his worn-out trowsers. Unlike Miss Herbey, his spirit seems to have sunk into apathy, and it is at times difficult to believe that he is living at all, so motionless and statue-like does he sit.

Silence continues to reign upon the raft. Not a sound, not even a groan, escapes our lips. We do not exchange ten words in the course of the day, and the few syllables that our parched tongue and swollen lips can pronounce are almost unintelligible. Wasted and bloodless, we are no longer human beings; we are spectres.

CHAPTER LI.

JANUARY 24th.—I have inquired more than once of Curtis if he has the faintest idea to what quarter of the Atlantic we have drifted, and each time he has been unable to give me a decided answer, though from his general observation of the direction of the wind and currents he imagines that we have been carried westwards, that is to say, towards the land.

To-day the breeze has dropped entirely, but the heavy swell is still upon the sea, and is an unquestionable sign that a tempest has been raging at no great distance. The raft labours hard against the waves, and Curtis, Falsten, and the boatswain, employ the little energy that remains to them in strengthening the joints. Why do they give themselves such trouble? Why not let the few frail planks part asunder, and allow the ocean to terminate our miserable existence? Certain it seems that our sufferings must have reached their utmost limit, and nothing could exceed the torture that we are enduring. The sky pours down upon us a heat like that of molten lead, and the sweat that saturates the tattered clothes that hang about our bodies goes far to aggravate the agonies of our thirst. No words of mine can describe this dire distress; these sufferings are beyond human estimate.

Even bathing, the only means of refreshment that we possessed, has now become impossible, for ever since Jynxstrop's death the sharks have hung about the raft in shoals.

To-day I tried to gain a few drops of fresh water by evaporation, but even with the exercise of the greatest patience, it was with the utmost difficulty that I obtained enough to moisten a little scrap of linen; and the only kettle that we had was so old and battered, that it would not bear the fire, so that I was obliged to give up the attempt in despair.

Falsten is now almost exhausted, and if he survives us at all, it can only be for a few days. Whenever I raised my head I always failed to see him, but he was probably lying sheltered somewhere beneath the sails. Curtis was the only man who remained on his feet, but with indomitable pluck he continued to stand on the front of the raft, waiting, watching, hoping. To look at him, with his unflagging energy, almost tempted me to imagine that he did well to hope, but I dared nor entertain one sanguine thought; and there I lay, waiting, nay, longing for death.

How many hours passed away thus I cannot tell, but after a time a loud peal of laughter burst upon my ear Some one else, then, was going mad, I thought; but the idea did not rouse me in the least. The laughter was repeated with greater vehemence, but I never raised my head. Presently I caught a few incoherent words.

"Fields, fields, gardens and trees! Look, there's an inn under the trees! Quick, quick! brandy, gin, water! a guinea a drop! I'll pay for it! I've lots of money! lots! lots!"

Poor deluded wretch! I thought again; the wealth of a nation could not buy a drop of water here. There was silence for a minute, when all of a sudden I heard the shout of "Land! land!"

The words acted upon me like an electric shock, and, with a frantic effort, I started to my feet. No land, indeed, was visible, but Flaypole, laughing, singing, and gesticulating, was raging up and down the raft. Sight, taste and hearing—all were gone; but the cerebral derangement supplied their place, and in imagination the maniac was conversing with absent friends, inviting them into the George Inn at Cardiff, offering them gin, whisky, and, above all water! Stumbling at every step, and singing in a cracked, discordant voice, he staggered about amongst us like an intoxicated man. With the loss of his senses all his sufferings had vanished, and his thirst was appeased. It was hard not to wish to be a partaker of his hallucination.

Dowlas, Falsten, and the boatswain, seemed to think that the unfortunate wretch would, like Jynxstrop, put an end to himself by leaping into the sea; but, determined this time to preserve the body, that it might serve a better purpose than merely feeding the sharks, they rose and followed the madman everywhere he went, keeping a strict eye upon his every movement.

But the matter did not end as they expected. As though he were really intoxicated by the stimulants of which he had been raving, Flaypole at last sank down in a heap in a corner of the raft, where he lay lost in a heavy slumber.

CHAPTER LII.

JANUARY 25th.—Last night was very misty, and for some unaccountable reason, one of the hottest that can be imagined. The atmosphere was really so stifling, that it seemed as if it only required a spark to set it alight. The raft was not only quite stationary, but did not even rise and fall with any motion of the waves.

During the night I tried to count how many there were now on board, but I was utterly unable to collect my ideas sufficiently to make the enumeration. Sometimes I counted ten, sometimes twelve, and although I knew that eleven, since Jynxstrop was dead, was the correct number, I could never bring my reckoning right. Of one thing I felt quite sure, and that was that the number would very soon be ten. I was convinced that I could myself last but very little longer. All the events and associations of my life passed rapidly through my brain, My country, my friends, and my family all appeared as it were in a vision, and seemed as though they had come to bid me a last farewell.

Towards morning I woke from my sleep, if the languid stupour into which I had fallen was worthy of that name. One fixed idea had taken possession of my brain; I would put an end to myself, and I felt a sort of pleasure as I gloated over the power that I had to terminate my sufferings. I told Curtis, with the utmost composure, of my intention, and he received the intelligence as calmly as it was delivered.

"Of course you will do as you please," he said; "for, my own part, I shall not abandon my post. It is my duty to remain here, and unless death comes to carry me away, I shall stay where I am to the very last."

The dull grey fog still hung heavily over the ocean, but the sun was evidently shining above the mist, and would, in course of time, dispel the vapour. Towards seven o'clock I fancied I heard the cries of birds above my head. The sound was repeated three times, and as I went up to the captain to ask him about it, I heard him mutter to himself,—

"Birds! why, that looks as if land were not far off."

But although Curtis might still cling to the hope of reaching land, I knew not what it was to have one sanguine thought. For me there was neither continent nor island; the world was one fluid sphere, uniform, monotonous, as in the most primitive period of its formation. Nevertheless it must be owned that it was with a certain amount of impatience that I awaited the rising of the mist, for I was anxious to shake off the phantom fallacies that Curtis's words had suggested to my mind.

Not till eleven o'clock did the fog begin to break, and as it rolled in heavy folds along the surface of the water, I could every now and then catch glimpses of a clear blue sky beyond. Fierce sunbeams pierced the cloud-rifts, scorching and burning our bodies like red-hot iron; but it was only above our heads that there was any sunlight to condense the vapour; the horizon was still quite invisible. There was no wind, and for half an hour longer the fog hung heavily round the raft; whilst Curtis, leaning against the side, strove to penetrate the obscurity. At length the sun burst forth in full power, and, sweeping the surface of the ocean, dispelled the fog, and left the horizon opened to our eyes.

There, exactly as we had seen it for the last six weeks, was the circle that bounded sea and sky, unbroken, definite, distinct as ever! Curtis gazed with intensest scrutiny, but did not speak a word. I pitied him sincerely, for he alone of us all felt that he had not the right to put an end to his misery. For myself I had fully determined that if I lived till the following day, I would die by my own hand. Whether my companions were still alive, I hardly cared to know; it seemed as though days had passed since I had seen them.

Night drew on, but I could not sleep for a moment. Towards two o'clock in the morning my thirst was so intense that I was unable to suppress loud cries of agony. Was there nothing that would serve to quench the fire that was burning within me? What if instead of drinking the blood of others I were to drink my own? It would be all unavailing, I was well aware, but scarcely had the thought crossed my mind, than I proceeded to put it into execution. I unclasped my knife, and, stripping my arm, with a steady thrust I opened a small vein. The blood oozed out slowly, drop by drop, and as I eagerly swallowed the source of my very life, I felt that for a moment my torments were relieved, But only for a moment; all energy had failed my pulses, and almost immediately the blood had ceased to flow.

How long it seemed before the morning dawned! and when that morning came it brought another fog, heavy as before that again shut out the horizon. The fog was hot as the burning steam that issues from a boiler. It was to be my last day upon earth, and I felt that I would like to press the hand of a friend before I died. Curtis was standing near, and crawling up to him, I took his hand in my own. He seemed to know that I was taking my farewell, and with one last lingering hope he endeavoured to restrain me. But all in vain, my mind was finally made up.

I should have like to speak once again to M. Letourneur, Andre and Miss Herbey, but my courage failed me. I knew that the young girl would read my resolution in my eyes, and that she would speak to me of duty and of

God, and of eternity, and I dared not meet her gaze; and I would not run the risk of being persuaded to wait until a lingering death should overtake me. I returned to the back of the raft, and after making several efforts, I managed to get on to my feet. I cast one long look at the pitiless ocean and the unbroken horizon; if a sail or the outline of a coast bad broken on my view, I believe that I should only have deemed myself the victim of an illusion; but nothing of the kind appeared, and the sea was dreary as a desert.

It was ten o'clock in the morning. The pangs of hunger and the torments of thirst were racking me with redoubled vigour. All instinct of self-preservation had left me, and I felt that the hour had come when I must cease to suffer. Just as I was on the point of casting myself headlong into the sea, a voice, which I recognized as Dowlas's; broke upon my ear.

"Captain," he said, "we are going to draw lots."

Involuntarily I paused; I did not take my plunge, but returned to my place upon the raft.

CHAPTER LIII.

JANUARY 26th.—All heard and understood the proposition; in fact, it had been in contemplation for several days, but no one had ventured to put the idea into words. However, it was done now; lots were to be drawn, and to each would be assigned his share of the body of the one ordained by fate to be the victim. For my own part, I profess that I was quite resigned for the lot to fall upon myself. I thought I heard Andre Letourneur beg for an exception to be made in favour of Miss Herbey, but the sailors raised a murmur of dissent. As there were eleven of us on board, there were ten chances to one in each one's favour, a proportion which would be diminished if Miss Herbey were excluded, so that the young lady was forced to take her chance among the rest.

It was then half-past ten, and the boatswain, who had been roused from his lethargy by what the carpenter had said, insisted that the drawing should take place immediately. There was no reason for postponing the fatal lottery. There was not one of us that clung in the least to life, and we knew that at the worst, whoever should be doomed to die, would only precede the rest by a few days, or even hours. All that we desired was just once to slake our raging thirst and moderate our gnawing hunger.

How all the names found their way to the bottom of a hat I cannot tell. Very likely Falsten wrote them upon a leaf torn from his memorandum-book. But be that as it may, the eleven names were there, and it was unanimously agreed that the last name drawn should be the victim.

But who would draw the names? There was hesitation for a moment; then, "I will," said a voice behind me. Turning round, I beheld M. Letourneur standing with outstretched hand, and with his long white hair falling over his thin livid face that was almost sublime in its calmness. I divined at once the reason of this voluntary offer; I knew that it was the father's devotion in self-sacrifice that led him to undertake the office.

"As soon as you please," said the boatswain, and handed him the hat.

M. Letourneur proceeded to draw out the folded strips of paper one by one, and after reading out aloud the name upon it, handed it to its owner.

The first name called was that of Burke, who uttered a cry of delight; then followed Flaypole and the boatswain. What his name really was I never could exactly learn. Then came Falsten, Curtis, Sandon. More than half had now been called, and my name had not yet been drawn. I calculated my remaining chance; it was still four to one in my favour.

M. Letourneur continued his painful task. Since Burke's first exclamation of joy not a sound had escaped our lips, but all were listening in breathless silence. The seventh name was Miss Herbey's, but the young girl heard it without a start. Then came mine, yes, mine! and the ninth was that of Letourneur.

"Which one?" asked the boatswain.

"Andre," said M. Letourneur.

With one cry Andre fell back senseless. Only two names now remained in the hat; those of Dowlas and of M. Letourneur himself.

"Go on," almost roared the carpenter, surveying his partner in peril as though he could devour him. M. Letourneur almost had a smile upon his lips, as he drew forth the last paper but one, and with a firm, unfaltering voice, marvelous for his age, unfolded it slowly, and read the name of Dowlas. The carpenter gave a yell of relief as he heard the word.

M. Letourneur took the last bit of paper from the hat, and without looking at it, tore it to pieces. But, unperceived by all but myself, one little fragment flew into a corner of the raft. I crawled towards it and picked it up. On one side of it was written Andr—; the rest of the word was torn away. M. Letourneur saw what I had done, and rushing towards me, snatched the paper from my hands, and flung it into the sea.

CHAPTER LIV.

JANUARY 26th.—I understood it all; the devoted father having nothing more to give, had given his life for his son.

M. Letourneur was no longer a human being in the eyes of the famished creatures who were now yearning to see him sacrificed to their cravings. At the very sight of the victim thus provided, all the tortures of hunger returned with redoubled violence. With lips distended, and teeth displayed, they waited like a herd of carnivora until they could attack their prey with brutal voracity; it seemed almost doubtful whether they would not fall upon him while he was still alive. It seemed impossible that any appeal to their humanity could, at such a moment, have any weight; nevertheless, the appeal was made, and, incredible as it may seem, prevailed.

Just as the boatswain was about to act the part of butcher, and Dowlas stood, hatchet in hand, ready to complete the barbarous work, Miss Herbey advanced, or rather crawled, towards them.

"My friends," she pleaded, "will you not wait just one more day? If no land or ship is in sight to-morrow, then I suppose our poor companion must become your victim. But allow him one more day; in the name of mercy I entreat, I implore you."

My heart bounded as she made her pitiful appeal. It seemed to me as though the noble girl had spoken with an inspiration on her lips, and I fancied that, perhaps, in super-natural vision she had viewed the coast or the ship of which she spoke; and one more day was not much to us who had already suffered so long, and endured so much.

Curtis and Falsten agreed with me, and we all united to support Miss Herbey's merciful petition. The sailors did not utter a murmur, and the boatswain in a smothered voice said,—

"Very well, we will wait till daybreak tomorrow," and threw down his hatchet.

To-morrow, then, unless land or a sail appear, the horrible sacrifice will be accomplished. Stifling their sufferings by a strenuous effort, all returned to their places. The sailors crouched beneath the sails, caring nothing about scanning the ocean. Food was in store for them to-morrow, and that was enough for them.

As soon as Andre Letourneur came to his senses, his first thought was for his father, and I saw him count the passengers on the raft. He looked puzzled; when he lost consciousness there had been only two names left in the hat, those of his father and the carpenter; and yet M. Letourneur and Dowlas were both there still. Miss Herbey went up to him and told him quietly that the drawing of the lots had not yet been finished. Andre asked no further question, but took his father's hand. M. Letourneur's countenance was calm and serene; he seemed to be conscious of nothing except that the life of his son was spared, and as the two sat conversing in an undertone at the back of the raft, their whole existence seemed bound up in each other.

Meantime, I could not disabuse my mind of the impression caused by Miss Herbey's intervention. Something told me that help was near at hand, and that we were approaching the termination of our suspense and misery; the chimeras that were floating through my brain resolved themselves into realities, so that nothing appeared to me more certain than that either land or sail, be they miles away, would be discovered somewhere to leeward.

I imparted my convictions to M. Letourneur and his son. Andre was as sanguine as myself; poor boy! he little thinks what a loss there is in store for him tomorrow. His father listened gravely to all we said, and whatever he might think in his own mind, he did not give us any discouragement; Heaven, he said, he was sure would still spare the survivors of the "Chancellor," and then he lavished on his son caresses which he deemed to be his last.

Some time afterwards, when I was alone with him, M. Letourneur whispered in my ear,—

"Mr. Kazallon, I commend my boy to your care, and mark you, he must never know—"

His voice was choked with tears, and he could not finish his sentence.

But I was full of hope, and, without a moment's intermission, I kept my eyes fixed upon the unbroken horizon, Curtis, Miss Herbey, Falsten, and even the boatswain, were also eagerly scanning the broad expanse of sea.

Night has come on; but I have still a profound conviction that through the darkness some ship will approach, and that at daybreak our raft will be observed.

CHAPTER LV.

JANUARY 27th.—I did not close my eyes all night, and was keenly alive to the faintest sounds, and every ripple of the water, and every murmur of the waves, broke distinctly on my ear. One thing I noticed and accepted as a happy omen; not a single shark now lingered-round the raft. The waning moon rose at a quarter to one, and through the feeble glimmer which she cast across the ocean, many and many a time I fancied I caught sight of the longed-for sail, lying only a few cables' lengths away.

But when morning came, the sun rose once again upon a desert ocean, and my hopes began to fade. Neither ship nor shore had appeared, and as the shocking hour of execution drew near, my dreams of deliverance melted away; I shuddered in my very soul as I was brought face to face with the stern reality. I dared not look upon the victim, and whenever his eyes, so full of calmness and resignation, met my own, I turned away my head. I felt choked with horror, and my brain reeled as though I were intoxicated.

It was now six o'clock, and all hope had vanished from my breast; my heart beat rapidly, and a cold sweat of agony broke out all over me. Curtis and the boatswain stood by the mast attentively scanning the horizon. The boatswain's countenance was terrible to look upon; one could see that although he would not forestall the hour, he was determined not to wait a moment after it arrived. As for the captain, it was impossible to tell what really passed within his mind; his face was livid, and his whole existence seemed concentrated in the exercise of his power of vision. The sailors were crawling about the platform, with their eyes gleaming, like wild beasts ready to pounce upon their devoted prey.

I could no longer keep my place, and glided along to the front of the raft. The boatswain was still standing intent on his watch, but all of a sudden, in a voice that made me start he shouted,—

"Now then, time's up!" and followed by Dowlas, Burke, Flaypole, and Sandon, ran to the back of the raft. As Dowlas seized the hatchet convulsively, Miss Herbey could not suppress a cry of terror. Andre started to his feet.

"What are you going to do to my father?" he asked in accents choked with emotion.

"My boy," said M. Letourneur, "the lot has fallen upon me, and I must die!"

"Never!" shrieked Andre, throwing his arms about his father, "They shall kill me first. It was I who threw Hobart's body into the sea, and it is I who ought to die!"

But the words of the unhappy youth had no other effect than to increase the fury of the men who were so staunchly bent upon their bloody purpose.

"Come, come, no more fuss," said Dowlas, as he tore the young man away from his father's embrace.

Andre fell upon his back, in which position two of the sailors held him down so tightly that he could not move, whilst Burke and Sandon carried off their victim to the front.

All this had taken place much more rapidly than I have been able to describe it. I was transfixed with horror, and much as I wished to throw myself between M. Letourneur and his executioners, I seemed to be rooted to the spot where I was standing.

Meantime the sailors had been taking off some of M. Letourneur's clothes, and his neck and shoulders were already bare.

"Stop a moment!" he said in a tone in which was the ring of indomitable courage. "Stop! I don't want to deprive you of your ration; but I suppose you will not require to eat the whole of me today."

The sailors, taken aback by his suggestion, stared at him with amazement.

"There are ten of you," he went on. "My two arms will give you each a meal; cut them off for to-day, and to-morrow you shall have the rest of me."

"Agreed!" cried Dowlas; and as M. Letourneur held out his bare arms, quick as lightning the carpenter raised his hatchet.

Curtis and I could bear this scene no longer; whilst we were alive to prevent it, this butchery should not be permitted, and we rushed forwards simultaneously to snatch the victim from his murderers. A furious struggle ensued, and in the midst of the MELEE I was seized by one of the sailors, and hurled violently into the sea.

Closing my lips, I tried to die of suffocation in the water; but in spite of myself, my mouth opened, and a few drops trickled down my throat.

Merciful Heaven! the water was fresh!

CHAPTER LVI.

JANUARY 27th CONTINUED.—A change came over me as if by miracle. No longer had I any wish to die, and already Curtis, who had heard my cries, was throwing me a rope. I seized it eagerly, and was hauled up on to the raft, "Fresh water!" were the first words I uttered.

"Fresh water?" cried Curtis, "why then, my friends, we are not far from land!"

It was not too late; the blow had not been struck, and so the victim had not yet fallen. Curtis and Andre (who had regained his liberty) had fought with the cannibals, and it was just as they were yielding to overpowering numbers that my voice had made itself heard.

The struggle came to an end. As soon as the words "Fresh water" had escaped my lips, I leaned over the side of the raft and swallowed the life-giving liquid in greedy draughts. Miss Herbey was the first to follow my example, but soon Curtis, Falsten, and all the rest were on their knees and drinking eagerly, The rough sailors seemed as if by a magic touch transformed back from ravenous beasts to human beings, and I saw several of them raise their hands to heaven in silent gratitude, Andre and his father were the last to drink.

"But where are we?" I asked at length.

"The land is there," said Curtis pointing towards the west.

We all stared at the captain as though he were mocking us; no land was in sight, and the raft, just as ever, was the centre of a watery waste. Yet our senses had not deceived us the water we had been drinking was perfectly fresh.

"Yes," repeated the captain, "land is certainly there, not more than twenty miles to leeward."

"What land?" inquired the boatswain.

"South America," answered Curtis, "and near the Amazon; no other river has a current strong enough to freshen the ocean twenty miles from shore!"

CHAPTER LVII.

JANUARY 27th CONTINUED.—Curtis, no doubt was right The discharge from the mouth of the Amazon is enormously large, but we had probably drifted into the only spot in the Atlantic where we could find fresh water so far from land. Yet land, undoubtedly was there, and the breeze was carrying us onwards slowly but surely to our deliverance.

Miss Herbey's voice was heard pouring out fervent praise to Heaven, and we were all glad to unite our thanksgivings with hers. Then the whole of us (with the exception of Andre and his father, who remained by themselves together at the stern) clustered in a group, and kept our expectant gaze upon the horizon.

We had not long to wait. Before an hour had passed Curtis, leaped in ecstasy and raised the joyous shout of "Land ahoy!"

* * * *

My journal has come to a close.

I have only to relate, as briefly as possible, the circumstances that finally brought us to our destination.

A few hours after we first sighted land the raft was off Cape Magoari, on the Island of Marajo, and was observed by some fishermen who, with kind-hearted alacrity picked us up, and tended us most carefully. They conveyed us to Para, where we became the objects of unbounded sympathy.

The raft was brought to land in lat. 0deg. 12min. N., so that since we abandoned the "Chancellor" we had drifted at least fifteen degrees to the south-west. Except for the influence of the Gulf Stream we must have been carried far, far to the south, and in that case we should never have reached the mouth of the Amazon, and must inevitably have been lost.

Of the thirty-two souls—nine passengers, and twenty-three seamen—who left Charleston on board the ship, only five passengers and six seamen remain. Eleven of us alone survive.

An official account of our rescue was drawn up by the Brazilian authorities. Those who signed were Miss Herbey, J. R. Kazallon, M. Letourneur, Andre Letourneur, Mr. Falsten, the boatswain, Dowlas, Burke, Flaypole, Sandon, and last, though not least,

"Robert Curtis, captain."

At Para we soon found facilities for continuing our homeward route. A vessel took us to Cayenne, where we secured a passage on board one of the steamers of the French Transatlantic Aspinwall line, the "Ville de St. Nazaire," which conveyed us to Europe.

After all the dangers and privations which we have undergone together, it is scarcely necessary to say that there has arisen between the surviving passengers of the "Chancellor" a bond of friendship too indissoluble, I believe, for either time or circumstance to destroy; Curtis must ever remain the honoured and valued friend of those whose welfare he consulted so faithfully in their misfortunes; his conduct was beyond all praise.

When we were fairly on our homeward way, Miss Herbey by chance intimated to us her intention of retiring from the world and devoting the remainder of her life to the care of the sick and suffering.

"Then why not come and look after my son?" said M. Letourneur, adding, "he is an invalid, and he requires, as he deserves, the best of nursing."

Miss Herbey, after some deliberation, consented to become a member of their family, and finds in M. Letourneur a father, and in Andre a brother. A brother, I say; but may we not hope that she may be united by a dearer and a closer tie, and that the noble-hearted girl may experience the happiness that so richly she deserves?